The Sherwood Ring

The
Sherwood
Ring

ELIZABETH MARIE POPE

Illustrated by Evaline Ness

Houghton Mifflin Company Boston

contents

The Girl on the Horse   1

The Scrap of Tartan   29

The Cipher Letter   72

The Bean Pot   113

The Punch Bowl   170

The Secrets   220

To Mary

The Girl on the Horse

ANYWAY, I said savagely to myself as I tried to lift a large and very clumsy suitcase down from the baggage rack, anyway, it *is* my father's old home, and I've always liked antiques, and I suppose an ancestral house is always more interesting than —

"Oh, drat it! Ouch!"

"If you'll allow *me*, miss," said the conductor reproachfully.

"Thank you . . . very kind of you . . . don't know why I can't seem to manage anything today. Are — are we getting near New Jerusalem yet?"

"Only about twenty minutes more now, miss."

Only about twenty minutes more.

Twenty minutes.

Feeling suddenly weak in the knees, I sank back on the hard train seat and glanced again at the gloomy landscape lumbering past the window. I had always heard that upper New York State was beautiful, but it certainly was not on a gray late afternoon in May, with the clouds blowing in rainy gusts off the low hills, and the barns and trees and little white farmhouses all huddled together as if trying to shelter themselves from the wet. The train window was so dank with mist anyway that it was hard to see anything at all except the reflection of my own dark figure hunched down under the baggage rack in my black tweed coat and hat.

The tweed coat had been green when my father bought it for me in London that spring, but the nice old landlady at the little Scottish inn where we were staying when he was taken ill had firmly sent it out to be dyed the day before the funeral.

"No doubt but that Ian MacDonald will make a poor hand of the dyeing," she had remarked, patting my shoulder in a motherly way; "but it will be ready the morn, and better for you than having no blacks for your father at all."

Ian MacDonald had indeed made but a poor hand of the dyeing. The coat had come home shrunken, curiously streaked and rusty looking, with two buttons broken. But it was black, undeniably black — and kind old Mrs. Campbell had looked so pleased over her thoughtfulness for me that I simply did not have the heart to tell her that nothing would have shocked my father more than the idea that I was wearing mourning for him at all.

The truth was that my father did not really like me very much. You could not blame him. An artist and a traveler, he should probably never have married at all — certainly he should never have been

2

left with a squalling newborn baby on his hands when my mother died. As long as he could afford it, he had merely dumped me on a succession of nurse-maids, schools, and camps while he wandered. When he could no longer afford it, he had taken me along with him on the strict understanding that I was to keep quiet and stay out from under his feet as much as possible. In all the seventeen years the only time he had ever spoken to me with any tenderness — if you could call it that — was the afternoon of the day before he died.

"I've been a bad father to you, Peggy," he had said suddenly, turning his head on the pillow to look at me. "I've — what's that expression Mrs. Campbell always uses? I've made but a poor hand of you."

"You haven't — you're not," I choked. "I never minded. I —"

"Don't talk nonsense!" said my father briskly. "If I hadn't been a selfish fool, there'd be enough money left to send you to college and get you fairly started in the world. As it is, I can't do anything except ship you back to Enos at Rest-and-be-thankful. I wrote to him yesterday after I saw the doctor. He'll be expecting you."

There was a blank pause while I tried to grasp what he was talking about. I was used to my father's casual way of announcing his plans ("You'd better pack your bags, Peggy; we're leaving for Italy in the morning"), but this was really a little too much.

"Enos — he's your older brother, isn't he?" I ventured at last. "I don't seem to remember anything about a place called Rest-and-be-thankful."

"Why should you?" my father snapped. "I never remember it myself when I can help it."

Then he grinned unexpectedly.

"You'd better not let Enos know I said that," he added. "He probably thinks I spent half my time holding you on my knee telling you fairy tales about the ancestral estate. That's the kind of man he is."

"Is Rest-and-be-thankful the ancestral estate?"

"In every sense of the word." My father made a face at the thought of it. "The first Enos Grahame — he was one of those impossible Highland chieftains who rebelled with Bonnie Prince Charlie and had to flee from Scotland in the customary fishing boat afterwards — the first Enos Grahame came to Orange County in New York and built the place in 1749, I think it was. He named it after that resting place on the hill at Edinburgh. The Grahames have been there ever since, accumulating family traditions. You probably know the sort of thing I mean."

"A bed George Washington slept in?"

"*Two* beds — he stayed with us twice. Also Lafayette, Alexander Hamilton, Benedict Arnold — no, I'm wrong, Benedict Arnold only came to dinner, but we still have the wineglass he drank from. There's even a rock in the garden Fenimore

4

Cooper is supposed to have stubbed his toe on during a garden party in 1842. I used to think I'd go crazy sometimes listening to your Uncle Enos moon about them all. The whole family were always a little beside themselves over Rest-and-be-thankful, but your Uncle Enos was the worst of the lot. Would you believe it? The last time I saw him, he said with a perfectly straight face that as long as he owned the place the first Enos Grahame could come back whenever he liked and find the whole house just as he remembered it! I told him I could think of better ways of spending my time than trying to make life comfortable for a pack of ghosts I couldn't even see. That did it!" My father chuckled unrepentantly. "Never saw Enos so mad in my life."

"Well, you have to admit it wasn't a very nice thing to say."

"That he was keeping a pack of ghosts? Oh, Enos wouldn't have minded that so much — matter of fact, he'd probably have taken it as a compliment, the fool! It's not being able to see them himself that gets under his skin. Well, if I were a ghost I don't know that I'd bother appearing to Enos either; but he seems to think that being the head of the family ought to have given him some sort of priority, and — the truth is, Peggy, if they *do* happen to get after you, it might be a good idea not to mention it. He'd never forgive you."

I could only stare at him helplessly.

"Well?" said my father. "What's the matter now?"

"But you're talking — " I gasped, "you're talking as if you thought Rest-and-be-thankful actually *is* haunted."

"Well," said my father, "it actually is, you know."

"But — " I began again.

"Never mind arguing about it now," my father interrupted me. "Wait till you see Rest-and-be-thankful; then you'll understand. And take that look off your face! They're not supposed to rattle chains or flap about wailing in misty sheets. All they do is come around sometimes when they happen to feel like it. You probably won't be able to see them anyway — Enos never has, and neither could I, though Great-Aunt Emily used to say that she got to know some of them quite well when she was a girl. And of course Louise was always trying to make out that she could see them too, but she was such an awful liar that I never believed a word of it."

"Who was Louise?"

"My little sister. You can forget about her. She got married a good many years ago and is making life miserable for some chapter of the D.A.R. out in the Middle West. She and Enos had a fight over one of the family tea sets she wanted to take with her, and he hasn't spoken to her since that I know of."

I gulped. It was beginning to sound as if a live

Uncle Enos would be even more difficult to get along with than a whole houseful of ghosts, even regular ghosts of the misty-sheet variety.

"Oh, he's all right if you just don't expect him to love you any better than a family tea set," was all the comfort my father gave me. "Of course, Enos always was a queer fish, and living alone so long with his everlasting antiques and family traditions has made him queerer than ever. But I don't think you have anything to worry about. I've brought you up not to be a nuisance; you ought to be able to look after yourself. You can't expect him to change his ways for you, of course. Just be quiet and don't bother him any more than you can help — Oh, that reminds me." He sat up suddenly against his pillows. "I told Enos in my letter that you were accustomed to looking after yourself and he needn't trouble about meeting you. Send him a telegram when you arrive at the airport and then take any train on the railroad that stops at a little place called New Jerusalem. That's where you get off."

New Jerusalem . . .

Only about twenty minutes more now.

"Excuse me, miss."

I looked up. The conductor was standing beside me again — a roly-poly little man with white hair who looked as if he wanted to smile but wasn't quite certain how I would take it. "Excuse me, miss," he repeated, "but would you by any chance be going to a place called Restenbeethankful?"

"Why, yes," I stammered. "Yes, but — I mean, how on earth did you happen to know?"

The conductor, his smile broadening, told me that I looked very much like my grandfather, who had gone fishing with him when they were boys, and also like my father, who had traveled up and down regularly on that particular train when he was at school and college.

"And it was that put me in mind of something I thought I'd better ask you, miss, just in case. Not that I want to butt in or anything, only — did you fix it up with your uncle to be met at the station?"

"No; I don't want to bother him. I was going to walk."

"Walk!" The conductor almost dropped his ticket punch. "But you can't be going to do that, miss! Why, it's six miles outa town, and wet, and back roads all the way."

"Six *miles?*" I could feel my heart like a lump of ice sliding down my backbone into my shoes.

"Six miles and a bit. More like seven."

I wondered desperately whether my remaining money would run to hiring a taxicab and decided that it would have to.

"But there ain't no taxi in New Jerusalem, miss," said the conductor when I asked him. "It's only a

8

little place, and most folks have cars. Ted Lowry at the garage used to keep an old Ford he hired out, but it breaks down more'n it runs, if you see what I mean, and anyway he's rented it now to some professor from England who's boarding at Mrs. Dykemann's. No — what I had in mind was that you might want to do what your father did back in the old days when he came home unexpected. Three forty-five we'd stop to pick up some milk off a loading platform, edge of Tatlock's big dairy farm. I'd take his bags on to New Jerusalem and he'd cut down through the hayfield to the road by Martin's Wood. It ain't more'n a mile and a half to Restenbeethankful that way."

"But surely trains don't stop to pick up milk along the tracks any more!" I protested.

The conductor looked at me for a moment and then slowly closed one eye.

"You just leave it to me, miss," he said. "We'll stop."

How he did it I never knew, but ten minutes later the train had stopped and I, with my overnight case, was scrambling out onto the old loading platform that stood by the tracks in Tatlock's hayfield. From the platform the remains of what had once been a wagon road sloped up the field to a gap in the low stone wall. The gap in turn led onto a country road that rambled away over the hill, hand in hand with

9

a noisy little brook. It had stopped raining, but the sky was still overhung with scudding dark clouds and all the ruts were full of water.

I went by two more fields and a pasture where an old white horse turned his head to look after me; then the country lifted and became wilder and more overgrown. The low stone walls disappeared or lay tumbled under clustering masses of blackberry and woodbine. The brook was lost in thickets of young trees. Presently leaves closed in about the road, branches began to meet overhead, and I found myself in a wood — or rather in something that looked like a forgotten corner of the original forest — huge elms and maples and mountainous oaks that must have been old when the first Enos Grahame was young. They were so dense that it was impossible to see more than a foot or two into the tangle on either side, and even where I stood it was almost dark.

I began to walk a little more quickly. It was getting late, and a ground mist had begun to rise from the dripping forest and was blowing vaporously across the road.

Then the road suddenly came to an end.

It was like a bad dream. One moment the road was there; the next it had split into two separate roads, one going off into the trees on the right and the other going off into the trees on the left. There was no signpost and no possible way of telling which branch led to Rest-and-be-thankful.

I came to a dead stop between the two, wondering frantically what on earth I was to do now. My hair was wet, and my feet were wet, and the overnight case was beginning to drag heavily on my arm. I tried to fling back my head bravely, but the gesture only brushed an overhanging branch and sent a shower of cold spray down the back of my neck. It was darker than ever under the trees, and I was sure that it would only be a matter of time before it started to rain again.

"Can I help you?" said a voice over my shoulder. "Have you lost your way?"

There behind me — apparently sprung out of nowhere — was a girl about my own age sitting sidesaddle on a tall black horse. She was wrapped in a long crimson raincape with a hood that was pulled down over her hair and shadowed her face, but even in the dim light and the mist I could see that it was a beautiful face, dark and proud, with wide-set gray eyes that were brilliant as jewels. It did flash through my mind that she was rather curiously dressed and it was strange that I had not heard the horse's hoofs coming up behind me on the road, but at the moment all I could really think was that here at last was somebody who might be able to tell me how to get out of the wood.

"Can I help you?" said the girl again.

"Oh *yes*, please, if you will," I answered gratefully. "I'm trying to walk to Rest-and-be-thankful,

and I don't know what turn I ought to take here."

The girl bent her head and sat for a moment as if she were considering something. Then she looked up, and tucking back a dark curl that was blowing out of her hood, she lifted her riding crop and pointed with it to the road on the left.

"A little past the first bend in *that* direction," she said, "you will come upon a young man repairing a small car which has broken down. I am sure that he would be glad to tell you the way to Rest-and-be-thankful if you asked him."

And without another word she touched her mount with her heel and went off down the road on the right. In another instant both she and the black horse had melted into the depths of the wood as noiselessly as shadows.

Then, as I stood rigid where she had left me, staring after her, utterly mystified, I realized that in spite of her strange appearance and behavior she had been right about one thing at least. There *was* somebody down the road to the left. Through the sighing of the wind and the mournful drip of the branches, I could hear a sharp clinking noise as one piece of metal struck another, and above it — faint but unmistakable — a man whistling a little tune. It was a catchy, swaggering air like an old ballad and it came dancing through the uncanny silences and shadows of the wood as comfortingly as an out-stretched hand.

I followed the sounds a little past the first bend of the road, and there — just as the girl on the horse had said — was a small and very shaky-looking old Ford in obvious difficulties. The hood was raised, and the whistler — a tall, fair young man with his shirt sleeves rolled up — was bending over the engine, doing something with a wrench and an oil can. The engine shuddered indignantly and then apparently lost consciousness again.

"Behave yourself, Betsy," said the young man in a severe voice. "Drink your nice oil, or — " He caught sight of me and straightened up with a jerk. "Good Lord, a human being!" he exclaimed. "Where did you come from? I beg your pardon," he added apologetically, "but I haven't seen anybody for so long that you took me by surprise."

"But didn't a girl in red go by you just a few minutes ago?" I asked. "She must have passed you. A girl in red, riding a black horse?"

The young man laughed and shook his head. "No, neither she nor yet a maharajah on a jeweled elephant," he said cheerfully. "There hasn't been anybody at all. What's the matter? Were you looking for her?"

"No; I just happened to meet her down the road. I was trying to get to a place called Rest-and-be-thankful and she thought that you could tell me the way."

14

"Now that I can do," said the young man. "I'm trying to get there myself, as a matter of fact. Unless Ted Lowry at the garage has played me false, it ought to be about a mile from here, straight ahead. But mayn't I give you a lift? I know your mother probably told you never to accept rides from questionable strangers, but I happen to be the dull, trustworthy type, and while I haven't my Boy Scout merit badges or my letter from the Vicar in my pocket just at the moment — "

"But I think I must have heard about you already," I interrupted. "Aren't you the professor from England who rented Ted Lowry's car and is boarding at Mrs. Dykemann's?"

"England, yes; professor, no — at least not for about another twenty years," said the young man. "It's nice to know that that's the way I impress people, but to tell the truth I'm just a student over here on a scholarship to do some research on your War of Independence. My name is Thorne; most of my friends call me Pat."

"Mine is Grahame — Peggy Grahame. Mr. Grahame at Rest-and-be-thankful is my uncle."

"He *is?*" The young man's eyes lit up. "Miss Grahame, I don't want to seem impertinent or — or intrusive, but would you mind very much if I asked you something? It's just that I can't understand the situation at all, and the fact is — Good

Lord, I'm keeping you waiting in the mud! Here, get in the car and put this over you; I think it's probably the original buffalo robe Ted Lowry's grandfather used when he went out courtin' in his cutter, but it may help to keep you warm."

"What were you going to say the fact was?" I asked, spreading the buffalo robe across my knees.

"That's the trouble — I don't know." Pat had returned to the engine and was poking at it rather savagely. "The whole business makes no sense at all. Did you ever read one of those mysteries where the heroine leaves her mother at the hotel for a few hours while she goes out to see the strange city, and when she comes back the mother has disappeared and the room has been refurnished and all the employees swear themselves blue that they never laid eyes on her before? I always used to think it was a silly sort of story myself. But now I'm not so sure."

"You mean you left your mother in a hotel, and —"

"Heavens, no! Only what's been happening to me is just a little too much like that story to be funny. Listen! I told you I was a student over here on a scholarship, didn't I? Well, I got it to do a history of guerrilla warfare in New York during the Revolution. I was particularly keen on the idea because one of the eighteenth-century Thornes was with the British army and is supposed to have been involved with the guerrillas in some way. I remem-

16

ber an old cousin of mine telling me about him once when I was a boy down at the family place on a holiday. He showed me his picture and a great pack of his letters and the diary he'd kept while he was serving in America. I didn't actually read them myself at the time — I couldn't have been more than ten — but I saw them. That I am certain of: *certain*."

"But why shouldn't you be?"

"That's just the point. When I heard about the scholarship, naturally the first thing I thought of was laying my hands on that stuff. It was original source material, you see, that had never been published; and since my cousin had said that the eighteenth-century Thorne was a rather remarkable man, it might very well turn out to be really important. My cousin had died that winter, and I'd inherited the place, but a sister of his who'd kept house for him was still living there. So I went down for a week before I sailed to say goodbye and make arrangements for taking the papers with me. And would you believe it? Cousin Mildred simply looked me in the eye and said her poor brother must have been making up bedtime stories to amuse me. There wasn't any picture. There wasn't any diary. There weren't any letters. There hadn't even been any eighteenth-century Thorne who'd fought in the War of Independence. And she would thank me to be a little more quiet and stop pestering her about it. No such person had ever existed, and the sooner I got that through my head the better it would be for all concerned. The worst of it was that as far as I could tell she was quite right."

"You mean you weren't able to find anything — anything at all?"

"Not a trace. Not a whiff. Not a scrap. And it wasn't as if I didn't take the house apart practically brick by brick looking for the stuff, either. There was just one hint I found that kept me from feeling I must be completely mad. The picture I told you about was only a little thing — one of those miniatures painted on ivory with a round gold frame — and my cousin had hung it on the wall beside the desk in his study. By the time I got there, it was gone like all the rest, of course; and a big Victorian water color of Salisbury Cathedral At Sunset was hanging in its place. But underneath there was a little round dark patch on the wallpaper, just the shape and size of the miniature as I remembered it. Something of the kind had certainly been there for years. Wait a minute. I think Betsy's coming out of her tantrum."

He drew down the hood of the car with great care, as if he were afraid of disturbing somebody, and slid cautiously under the wheel. Betsy coughed once or twice in a fretful way and began to snuffle forward.

"What did your Cousin Mildred say when you told her about finding the place for the miniature?"

"She said that if I thought I could hold her accountable for every spot on the wallpaper, I was mistaken, and her sainted mother had painted the water color of Salisbury Cathedral At Sunset with her own hands, and it was very fortunate she wasn't back on earth today to see what the manners of the younger generation had come to. At that point, I gave up. My ship was due to sail in a couple of days, and I decided I might as well let the whole Mildred problem wait till I saw what I could find at this end. My late cousin had said something about the eighteenth-century Thornes being connected in some way with the Grahames at Rest-and-be-thankful — I'd remembered the name because it was so odd — and I thought your uncle might be able to help me out. I particularly wanted to get in touch with him anyway, because everybody had told me that he was *the* authority on local history in Orange County and couldn't be kinder or more generous about letting young scholars consult him and work with his collections. Kind and generous — those were the exact words." Pat scowled furiously, and Betsy, apparently taking his expression as a personal insult, let out a squeal and collapsed again.

"But what happened?" I demanded, when we were moving once more.

"I don't know, I tell you! It was the business with Cousin Mildred all over again, only worse. I wrote him politely when I got in, enclosing my letters of introduction and asking when it would be convenient for me to call. He didn't answer. I wrote him again, and he still didn't answer. I tried telephoning, but the operator says he doesn't have a telephone. Finally, I decided that the only thing left to do was drive out and make one last effort to see him myself. Not that I expect this will work, either, but — look here, Miss Grahame, what's the matter with me? What's wrong? Do you happen to know if I've done anything to offend your uncle? Or is this just the way he usually behaves?"

I was obliged to tell him that I had no more idea than he had of the way Uncle Enos usually behaved, but added soothingly that there had probably been some simple misunderstanding, and everything would be cleared up as soon as we got to Rest-and-be-thankful.

"I certainly hope so," said Pat gloomily. "I'm beginning to feel like one of those characters who's under a mysterious family curse."

"The sun's coming out again, anyway," I went on. "Maybe it's a good omen. The woods seem to be getting thinner, too, and — oh, look! Look there!"

The last of the trees had fallen away behind us, and the road was dipping down into a little valley that lay between two curving hills, a valley full of apple trees, all in full bloom — immense, straggling apple trees, the largest and oldest I had ever seen. Where the two hills met, there rose suddenly from

the drifts of delicate flowers, as if from some enchanted sea, the mossy dark roof of a huge stone
house. There were four enormous chimneys, two
at each of the main gables, and between them along
the ridgepole perched three white pigeons, sunning
themselves after the rain. Below, there were
glimpses through the foaming branches of weath-
ered stone walls and dark shutters.

I had never been in a place that looked so quiet,
so utterly hushed. No one was in sight; not a leaf
stirred or a voice broke the golden stillness that lay
like a spell over everything. Even the pigeons on
the roof sat without cooing or preening, the afternoon light gleaming on their motionless feathers.

"So that was why they called it Rest-and-be-thankful," I murmured. For some reason I did not feel
as if I ought to raise my voice.

"Betsy seems to think so, anyway," said Pat ruefully. "She's stopping again."

This time Betsy had apparently settled down for
a long nap, and it proved impossible to rouse her.
In the end, Pat took my overnight case and we
walked down the driveway under the apple trees
and on through a velvet-like formal garden to the
house. There, four steps led up to a flagged terrace
with a balustrade and great urns heaped with trailing ivy and rose geranium.

"You know, I'm inclined to think that poor Betsy
was just trying to be tactful," said Pat, glancing up

21

at the fanlight and the fluted white columns of the doorway. "This isn't the kind of setting where she looks her best. We really ought to be arriving in a coach and four, with outriders and powdered footmen up behind."

At that moment the door opened and a very old butler with white hair bowed to me, saying something in a voice which shook so that I could only distinguish the words "Miss Peggy" and "come in" and "a great day for the house." Behind him was a wide shadowy hall with a grandfather clock that ticked loudly in the stillness and a huge fireplace with a trophy of guns and swords over the mantel. At the back a vast mahogany staircase went up into gloom.

"Mr. Enos is in the study," said the old butler, opening a door at the right. "He's been expecting you."

We passed into a dim, paneled library with high bookcases that reached to the ceiling and across it to another door on the far side. My heart was beginning to beat thunderously and my feet kept stumbling over each other. I glanced frantically around for Pat, but he only caught my eye and winked at me outrageously.

"Miss Peggy, sir," said the butler.

Uncle Enos was sitting in a high-backed wing chair by the fire. I recognized him instantly: very tall, very dark, very slender, with what we called "the Grahame face" — long and narrow, the thin straight black eyebrows over wide-set gray eyes, like my father's and my own. But my father had never stood so erect, or carried himself with such overwhelming dignity. When Uncle Enos came forward and held out his hand to me, it was almost as if he were tossing a ruffle of lace back from his wrist.

"My dear child," he said magnificently.

He sounded so like a character in an eighteenth-century novel that I felt I really ought to sink down in a deep curtsey and ask him for his blessing. As it was, I merely found myself touching his hand for a brief instant and murmuring something about being glad to see him. Uncle Enos in return expressed the polite hope that I had not had too long or difficult a journey. "But I see," he added, "that you were traveling with friends?" — and his eyes went inquiringly to Pat standing near the door.

Pat set down the overnight case and took a determined step forward.

"My name is Thorne, sir," he said clearly, "and I have been very eager to meet you for a long time now."

I had wondered what was going to happen when Pat and Uncle Enos finally came together, but not even in my wildest speculations had I hit upon the sort of thing that actually occurred. Uncle Enos stared at him for one stupefied instant, and then said in the most appalling voice:

23

"You!"

"Why, yes, I suppose so," said poor Pat, utterly taken aback. "You remember that I wrote you some time ago for information in connection with my study of guerrilla warfare in Orange County during the —"

Uncle Enos merely drew himself up in front of his desk as if he were bodily trying to protect its contents from the contamination of Pat's glance.

"I have nothing whatever to say to you, sir," he interrupted him in a voice of ice. "You will leave this house at once."

And with that he actually stretched out his arm and pointed his finger at the door, exactly like the outraged father in an old steel engraving called "Her Tory Lover" that I remembered hanging on the wall of Mrs. Campbell's inn parlor.

"Uncle Enos, please!" I clutched at his other arm desperately. "Please! You don't understand. This gentleman has been very kind to me. He —"

"Be quiet, child!" Uncle Enos made a fierce gesture with his free hand. "Let me deal with this! I don't know how he contrived to make your acquaintance, but you are never to have anything more to do with him. Never, do you hear me?"

"But why, Uncle Enos? Why? What is it? What is he supposed to have done?"

"Yes, if you don't mind, sir, what *am* I supposed to have done?" Pat cut in. "Look, Mr. Grahame, I'm sure that there must be some mistake. If you'll only explain — "

"I have no explanation to offer you, now or on any future occasion," announced Uncle Enos grandly. "I have told you to leave my house, and I have told my niece she is not to see you again. That is enough for you both. I refuse to discuss the subject any further." He flung back his head, standing very straight, one hand at his hip as if it were resting on the hilt of a sword. He looked more like an eighteenth-century gentleman than ever.

But Pat was beginning to lose his own temper and look rather like an eighteenth-century gentleman himself — the haughty young officer in "Her Tory Lover," in fact. He did not rage or stamp or shout. He simply allowed his gaze to rest on Uncle Enos as if he were seeing him from somewhere a long way off and did not find him particularly attractive.

"In that case, sir," he retorted, "I think there is nothing more I have to say to you, except perhaps — " he turned with his hand on the knob of the door and grinned at Uncle Enos impertinently, "that I have every intention of seeing your niece again, very soon, whether you like it or not." Then he was gone.

As the door swung shut behind him, Uncle Enos suddenly began to shake. He caught rather fumblingly at the back of his desk chair and sank down into it, almost as though he could no longer stand.

"What shall I do now?" he whispered. "What on earth shall I do?" He was speaking to himself — apparently he did not even realize that I was still in the room — and his face looked so white and miserable that I could not help going to him and putting my hand on his shoulder.

"Dear Uncle Enos," I begged, "can't you possibly tell me what's the matter?"

But Uncle Enos was already recovering himself. He twitched his shoulder away from my touch and pulled his chair around to the desk, turning his back on me altogether.

"I thought I told you I was not going to discuss the subject." He reached for his pen and letter pad with an impatient jerk. "Run along now like a good child, and don't bother me. I have work to do. If you'll just go back to the hall and speak to the butler, he'll take you up to your room."

The butler, however, had gone away and there was nobody in the hall when I came out but a maid winding the grandfather clock — a very pretty girl in a long, full-skirted dress of flowered chintz with a ruffled cap and an organdy apron. She told me her name was Petunia, and she was the "downstairs" maid at Rest-and-be-thankful. She had an older sister, Zinnia, who attended to the "upstairs," and a younger sister, Gladiola, who helped the cook in the kitchen. All three were daughters of the butler, Christopher Seven — so called because he was de-

horse. She must live somewhere around here . . .
he probably knows who she is.

But as it turned out, I did not have to ask Uncle
Enos after all. The next moment I had come around
the bend of the stair into the landing; and there,
gleaming down from the paneled wall, hung a great
life-size portrait in a carved and gilded frame. It was
the portrait of a girl wearing a long crimson cloak
— a beautiful girl, dark and proud, with wide-set
gray eyes that were brilliant as jewels. One of her
hands rested on the shoulder of a tall black horse,
just visible behind her in the shadows; the other
hand was lifted to tuck back a dark curl that was
blowing out of her hood. On the frame under the
picture was a small square plaque with an inscrip-
tion:

BARBARA GRAHAME
At the Age of Sixteen
Painted by
John Singleton Copley
1773

I stood staring at the portrait for a long time
before I could get it through my head that I had
already met my first ghost at Rest-and-be-thankful.

scended from the original Christopher who had been butler in the days of the first Enos Grahame and had died in 1792, leaving a son, Christopher Two, and a grandson, Christopher Three, to carry on the line. The present Christopher was the seventh and last of the family. "And Mr. Enos has gone and got him so stuck-up about that name that he won't even let his own children call him Daddy no more," concluded Petunia, with a disrespectful giggle. "Did you say you wanted to go up to your room now, Miss Peggy? Dinner won't be till seven o'clock if you'd like to lie down a while first. You must be mighty tired after all that trip."

Suddenly I realized that I *was* tired — cruelly tired — so tired that it seemed a long way across the hall to the stairs. The strain and excitement and confusion of the afternoon had worn me out completely. Everything that had happened was whirling and jumbling incoherently through my mind — the walk through Martin's Wood; the mysterious girl on the horse; Pat and the curious story he had told me; my first glimpse of Rest-and-be-thankful among the apple trees; the scene in the study when Uncle Enos had so strangely refused to have anything more to do with Pat and had driven him out of the house . . .

Maybe it will get clearer tomorrow, I thought foggily as I trailed behind Petunia up the stairs Anyway, I can ask Uncle Enos about the girl on th

The Scrap of Tartan

I WAS SITTING on the floor in the library at Rest-and-be-thankful, sulking. Theoretically I was tidying up the bottom drawer of the big Chippendale cabinet, but actually I was sulking. Outside the sun was shining and the birds were singing and the open windows were clustered round with yellow roses — it was now three weeks since my arrival and we were well into June— but I was in no mood to do anything but sit on the floor with my back to the garden and think bitterly about my wrongs and grievances. There were a great many of them; and I was getting a certain miserable satisfaction from laying them all out and rummaging through them over and over again.

It was all very well for my father to say that I couldn't expect Uncle Enos to change his ways on my account. But surely my father had not supposed that Uncle Enos was going to behave as if he hardly knew I was even in the house? After three weeks I was still no better acquainted with him than I had been at the beginning. In fact, I almost never saw him except at meals, which were eaten in state at a long walnut table designed for twenty, with an enormous centerpiece of antique crystal and silver to conceal anyone sitting at one end from his companion at the other. Uncle Enos would come wandering in on the last stroke of the gong, with a book under his arm, say "Good morning" or "Good evening" absent-mindedly to me, prop open the book in front of him, and read it (as far as I could judge for the distance and the centerpiece) throughout the meal. The rest of the day he usually spent working in his study, and when interrupted would simply tell me over his shoulder to run along and stop bothering him.

Where was I to run to? What was I to do with myself? There was always the house to explore, of course — and I had to admit that Rest-and-be-thankful was a wonderful house — but what was the use of finding all sorts of fascinating things if I didn't know what they meant and the only person who could tell me wouldn't take the trouble?

That scrap of tartan, for instance.

I had just come across the scrap of tartan as I was turning out the bottom drawer of the Chippendale cabinet. It was a very small scrap, and looked as if it had been torn roughly out of a much larger piece like a kilt or a plaid. Somebody, perhaps a hundred years before, had pinned it carefully to a sheet of letter paper that was now dry and rustling with old age. Written across the paper, in brown faded ink, was one line — a verse from the Bible: "Pride goeth before destruction, and a haughty spirit before a fall." The writer had then added three exclamation marks, and drawn a small hand in the margin with one finger pointed warningly upward at the scrap of tartan.

It was not a scrap of the Grahame tartan. The colors and design — what old Mrs. Campbell in Scotland had called "the sett" — were quite different. Ours was very dark — mostly dull greens and blacks on a ground of deep blue. This was bright scarlet, with a dazzling pattern of yellows and whites and greens that must once have fairly glittered in the sun. If it was not ours, then whose was it? Why had it been so carefully kept all these years? Uncle Enos, of course, probably knew. I looked longingly across the room at the door of the study; but the door of the study was firmly shut, and I knew it would be useless to knock. Uncle Enos didn't want me bothering him. Nobody wanted me bothering him. Even Pat —

I threw the scrap of tartan back where I had found it and shut the drawer of the cabinet with a savage bang. Pat was the real trouble. I could have put up with Uncle Enos and the study door and the dining-room table and all the rest, if it only hadn't been for Pat.

Pat had said quite distinctly before he went away

that he was going to see me again very soon, whether Uncle Enos liked it or not. And I had been fool enough to believe him. I had watched the mail for days. I had found myself wandering casually time and again up through the orchard to the gate and leaning there almost as if I were waiting for somebody. But he had never come back. There had not even been a word from him.

Well, if that was the way he wanted it, why should I worry myself about him? Probably he had never really liked me at all, and only said he was going to see me again because he knew it would annoy Uncle Enos. Or did he by any chance suppose that he could simply turn up any time it happened to suit his convenience and find me there patiently leaning on the gate until he condescended to notice me? Well, he couldn't. I had my pride. It would be very easy to forget him completely if I chose. And he needn't think he could whistle me back whenever he wanted to, either. I could ignore other people myself, if it came to that, and keep them waiting about for weeks. I could treat him just as badly as he had treated me, and maybe that would show him —

"Show him what, exactly?" inquired a voice from the other side of the room.

For one dreadful moment I thought I had been speaking aloud, and that Uncle Enos had come out of his study to demand just why I was planning to have anything more to do with Pat at all? Then I realized that the study door was still fast shut, and there was nobody at that end of the library.

"Over here," said the voice.

Behind me, in the shadows by the fireplace, a tall young man was lounging in the deep armchair with his legs crossed and one booted foot resting on the fender. He had a dark, rather disdainful face, which was saved from absolute haughtiness only by a certain good humor about the eyes and mouth. His long cloak was untied and flung back over his shoulders, and underneath it I could see that he was wearing the buff-and-blue uniform and gold epaulets of an officer in the Continental Army. The uniform looked very shabby: the right sleeve had been awkwardly darned, and the boot resting on the fender was patched.

"Well, Peggy," said the young man, with a sudden delightful smile that changed his arrogant face completely. "Do you know who I am?"

I thought a moment. I had, as a matter of fact, recognized him at once, but it seemed rude to use the actual word "ghost."

"I believe there's a picture of you in the dining room hanging over the sideboard," I ventured at last. "You're the second Richard Grahame, aren't you, the one who was Barbara's brother? Only in the picture you seem younger, somehow, and of course you were dressed quite differently."

The second Richard Grahame laughed. "I was indeed," he said a little ruefully. "I used to think about that picture sometimes when I was sitting over a campfire, gnawing on a bone. Gray velvet with gold embroidery, wasn't it, and my nose in the air to show what a fine young gentleman I was? I almost took it down and hid it away when I came home after the war, but in the end I left it where it was to remind me of the fool I'd been. I kept the scrap of tartan too, and the — "

"You mean that scrap of tartan I found in the Chippendale cabinet?"

"That was the one."

"And it was you who wrote the line on the sheet of paper?"

" 'Pride goeth before destruction and a haughty spirit before a fall'? Oh, yes. My old tutor once made me copy that verse three hundred times when I was a boy as a warning to mend my ways before it was too late — and after what happened to me, I thought I might just as well copy it down again."

"But what *did* happen to you?" I demanded eagerly.

It's a sad story (said the second Richard Grahame), but I suppose it wouldn't have been quite so sad if I hadn't had what my Scottish grandmother called a good conceit of myself to begin with. You remember the dashing young gentleman in the dining room, with his velvet coat and his nose in the air? Well, I had to give up the coat when I went into the Army, of course, but I contrived to keep the nose for a considerable time after that. I had rather more than my share of good fortune in the field too, and it naturally did nothing to cure me. So I was a dashing young hero at the battle of Saratoga; and then I was a dashing young aide-de-camp for Israel Putnam when he commanded the fort at West Point; and then in the early summer of '79 I was a dashing young colonel riding downriver under orders to report for special duty to General Washington himself at headquarters. I am afraid that I must have been a little lofty in my manner to the elderly major and the middle-aged captain who were traveling with me. Poor things, they were obviously never going to be dashing young officers required for special duty by the commander-in-chief himself.

I found the commander-in-chief at his headquarters, with a sheaf of reports spread over the table before him, and a large map of New York pinned to the wall behind. He took a moment to welcome me kindly, and speak of a visit he had once paid my father at Rest-and-be-thankful. For all his graciousness I thought he seemed preoccupied and even troubled.

"You have been recommended to me, Colonel Grahame, as an officer with the ability and intelligence needed to carry out an exceedingly important mission."

He paused to look down at the papers in front of him, and I hurriedly adjusted my face to express the proper combination of gratitude, zeal, self-confidence, and courage.

"For the past few weeks, Colonel Grahame, reports of the most alarming nature have been coming in from your particular district of Orange County. It appears that during the last month or so the British have sent one of their young officers into the region with orders to assemble a gang of deserters, dispossessed loyalists, and secret Tories of all sorts to prey on patriot holdings, supply-trains for the army, isolated outposts, and the like. Such gangs, of course, are unfortunately only too common in that neighborhood, but most of them are too small and badly organized to be anything more than a nuisance. This one is different. It is under the command of a trained officer, who is also by all accounts a man of very singular competence and ingenuity. He hides out somewhere in the hills with a small band of permanent followers; but his real strength lies in his many secret friends and helpers among the valley farmers of the district, who keep him supplied with information and join him whenever he needs extra men for large raids or expeditions. On such occasions, they all wear masks to prevent recognition, and return home quietly afterwards to go on with their usual work until the next call. Their organization and system of communication is evidently something remarkable, as you will admit when I tell you that so far the local authorities have not been able to identify a single member of the gang except those actually killed or captured during attacks — many of them men who had been regarded as strong patriots for years."

"These prisoners could not be forced to tell the names of their companions, sir, or the hiding place of their leader?"

"They did not know themselves. That is an example of what I meant when I spoke of the leader's singular competence and ingenuity. I may add that this young man has already done much more damage than we can afford, and seems to be growing in strength and audacity every day. You understand now, I hope, the gravity — the extreme gravity — of the situation?"

I understood only too well not merely what General Washington was saying, but a good deal that he was leaving unsaid. Loose bands of marauders had long been the curse of our part of the country, bordering as it did on the dreadful "Neutral Ground" that lay between the British army holding New York City and the American army holding the north of the state. But such gangs were usually made up of ordinary ragamuffins out for loot, led by desperadoes like Claudius Smith and his three sons, who used the war simply as an excuse to plunder both sides with fine impartiality — men so lawless that no decent Tories would join them, even when they had no other way of striking a blow for the king. The British, praise be, could not or would not learn to make use of the thousands of loyalists scattered throughout the country. No American was permitted to join the regular army. If he chose to abandon his home and make the long, dangerous journey to New York, he had a thin chance of obtaining a place in one of the slipshod and badly handled Tory regiments slowly taking shape there — and many desperate or courageous loyalists took the chance. But many more lukewarm or cautious loyalists stayed where they were. Men with families they dared not leave behind or possessions they refused to give up, outwardly patriotic, outwardly resigned to the new government; inwardly resentful, and ready to make any mischief they could without losing their property or sinking to the level of common thieves. This new leader's plan sounded like exactly the sort of thing they had been waiting for. And if it once proved successful, if the British authorities were once convinced that it would work, then it might spread like an epidemic throughout the whole country — and the harm it could do was beyond calculation. I looked aghast at General Washington as the full extent of the danger became clear to me. He answered the look.

"If this business isn't stopped," he said, suddenly and violently, "stopped *now,* before it does any more damage, even as big a fool as General Sir Henry Clinton will be forced to realize the possibilities of it, and then — " he broke off with a little gesture of his hand as if he were throwing something away, "it may lose the war for us."

There was no answer I could make to that. I knew that what he had said was true as well as he did. "At least, it hasn't gone very far yet," was all the comfort I could think of.

"Neither has a forest fire — the first hour after it starts," retorted the General grimly. "All you have to do is get there and put it out in time." Then, as suddenly as it had risen, his voice became level and commanding again. "I have ordered thirty volunteers detached for special duty from Ogden Van Spurter's company of rangers. With these, you, Colonel Grahame, will proceed at once to Orange County and take whatever measures you think necessary to put a permanent end to these marauders. Those are the only men I can spare, and the only orders I can give you. The details I will leave to your own judgment — and I hope for the sake of your country that it is a sound one. Edward Shipley near New Jerusalem has very generously offered us his lands for your base and his own house for your headquarters. He is one of our most ardent patriots, and you may trust him as you would me."

My face fell. It was not that I distrusted old Mr. Shipley — I had known the whole family ever since I was a boy — but I did not find myself taking very greatly to the idea of camping at the Shipley Farm. I wanted to live at home, for one thing; and for another, I had a particular dislike of Mr. Shipley's daughter Eleanor, a rude, scrawny, redheaded little girl with a fleering tongue.

"Rest-and-be-thankful would be three miles nearer New Jerusalem, sir," I ventured to suggest deferentially.

General Washington nodded. "Yes," he said. "I'd thought of that. But your father writes that now that you and he are both away with the army, and the neighborhood in such an unsettled condition, he has decided to close the house altogether and send your sister to live with her aunt at New Jerusalem. It seems that your aunt is an invalid who feels the want of company, and your sister will of course be much safer and happier there."

That only showed how little General Washington knew about my Aunt Susanna, an old tyrant suffering from twenty-seven different diseases, of which twenty-five were imaginary and the other two entirely brought on by fretfulness and self-indulgence.

"I take it," the General was adding, "that you have no objection to the Shipley Farm itself."

I could not very well inform him that what I actually objected to was living under the same roof with an unmannerly, disrespectful brat like little Eleanor Shipley.

"No, sir," I murmured, as civilly as I could.

"Then we may regard it as settled, and there is no reason why you should not set out as soon as you can. Unless there is any further information you would like before you go?"

"Only about this British officer who's supposed to be leading the marauders, sir. I gather that he's the real heart and soul of all the trouble. Is anything more definitely known about him?"

"Not very much. He holds the rank of captain, and his name is Sherwood — Peaceable Drummond Sherwood, if that means anything to you. I thought parents in England had stopped giving their children names like 'Peaceable' a hundred years ago. Do you suppose his mother could have been a Quaker lady from Nantucket?"

"The 'Drummond' sounds more as if she were Scottish, sir."

"Perhaps. Ogden Van Spurter may be able to tell you. It appears that he actually met and talked to this Captain Sherwood when he went to New York on some military mission last winter. To be frank with you, I thought very seriously of giving this command to him — but he does not, of course, possess your intimate knowledge of the country, and the members of my staff who had worked with you both seemed to consider you the better man of the two."

That was not really quite so much of a compliment as it sounded. Ogden Van Spurter — known less formally as "Old Sputters" — was a young officer I disliked excessively, a thickheaded Hudson River Dutchman who had to be promoted because he was so brave and then watched ever afterwards because he was so stupid. I tried dutifully to find him that night and discover what he knew about Peaceable Sherwood, but he kept himself out of my way (sulking, I was told, over the loss of the command), and I did not see him until I left camp with my thirty the following morning. General Washington, taking an early ramble around the fortifications with a parcel of officers, came upon our little column headed west for the river, and halted it a moment to say goodbye and wish me luck. Sputters was glowering at his elbow, and I had the satisfaction of saluting him cheerfully as the General turned aside and we clattered off in a cloud of dust.

If the three Fates had suddenly appeared before me on the road, and solemnly warned me that this was to be my last happy moment for many months to come, I think I should have laughed in their faces. I was in a mood to laugh at everything that morning. I had been trusted with what General Washington himself had called "an exceedingly important mission." I was on my way home, even if the house was shut up and poor Barbara cast away in New Jerusalem with my Aunt Susanna. I was escaping from the grinding monotony of life at West Point, with its drill and discipline and everlasting superior officers. With any luck, I could probably manage to spend at least a week or so in Orange County hunting Peaceable Sherwood and his marauders. Peaceable Sherwood himself sounded as if he would make an entertaining antagonist. I was looking forward to the sport of running him down.

Even the prospect of camping at the Shipley Farm was beginning to seem less objectionable than it had at first. I had always liked the house — a pleasant, rambling, white place set in green meadows where Barbara and I had gone as children to hunt wild strawberries with little Eleanor Shipley. And, after all, who was little Eleanor Shipley that she should trouble me now? Her manners had probably improved in the six years which had gone by since I had seen her last. It was ridiculous to behave as if I were still the boy she could skin alive with a mere flicker of her sarcastic tongue. There was really no problem whatever. All I had to do was to be very formal, very distant, very courteous, and make her sorry that she had ever jeered at the dashing young hero who was going to save the whole cause of independence practically singlehanded. And when I had captured Peaceable Sherwood by some brilliant feat of arms, and rid the surrounding countryside of his marauders, then maybe she would realize —

"Colonel Grahame?" The lieutenant of the rangers had come up beside me and was clearing his throat.

"Did you say we were going to make camp at the Shipley Farm, sir?"

"Yes, why? Is anything the matter?"

Lieutenant Felton cleared his throat again. "It's only that we seem to have ridden right past it," he pointed out, apologetically. "There was a house and a big meadow back aways on the left, with the gates open and a girl calling after us when we went by."

I came out of my happy dreams with a jolt. There behind me, a good quarter of a mile down the road, were the white gates of the Shipley Farm; and beside them, standing on the lowest rail of the fence, was a little figure in blue which even at that distance looked distressingly familiar.

There was nothing I could do but wheel my horse around in dignified silence and start back again. Lieutenant Felton and twenty-nine mounted rangers also wheeled their horses around and followed me solemnly down the road to the gate.

It was Eleanor Shipley standing there, beyond a doubt. In the last six years she had somehow lost her scrawniness, and the bright hair blowing in little curls about her forehead was pure coppery gold; but she was still very small — so tiny that I could have swung her off her feet with one hand — and the mocking mouth I had so often longed to slap was just as I remembered it. She was perched on the rail as lightly as a butterfly, with a perfectly grave face, watching our approach with wide, innocent eyes. I remembered that look, too.

"Oh, Dick *dear!*" she said as I came up, her voice quivering with laughter. "What in the world happened to you? I quite thought you had forgotten us altogether."

I told myself firmly that all I had to do was to be very formal, very distant, very courteous, and let her see that she could no longer trifle with me.

"I was thinking, Miss Shipley," I explained, coldly. Then, as this seemed rather inadequate, I added in my loftiest tones, "There is, of course, a great deal weighing on my mind just now."

Eleanor merely continued to look at me for a moment.

"Ah, yes, I see," she remarked softly. "The dashing young hero who is going to save the whole cause of independence singlehanded." She had always had the most detestable habit of putting into exact words a number of thoughts which I would much rather have kept all vague and warm and unspoken in the most secret chambers of my mind.

For one passionate moment I found myself wishing I was fourteen again, so I could pick her up like a kitten and scrub her face with mud to teach her manners, the way I had done the last time she had tried that trick on me. But a full-blown colonel with a company at his back could only wrap himself in the tattered remains of his dignity, and turn pointedly away from her to speak to Mr. Shipley, who was hobbling down the drive as fast as he could come, his kind old face beaming with welcome and delight.

"My boy, my dear boy!" he cried, reaching up to clasp my hand. "Bless my soul, how you've grown! Eleanor, isn't he a fine, dashing young man? This is a great day for the county. I was here at the gate to meet you, but I'd just stepped back to the house a moment to fetch these letters that came for you this morning. Eleanor has been watching the road since dawn" — ("To get the first bite?" I wondered bitterly) — "and you'll find firewood and forage all prepared for you in the South Meadow. We've given you the bedroom on the ground floor, off the parlor, where you can come and go as you like. Bless my soul, it seems only yesterday that you were falling out of that oak in the South Meadow! And now! Eleanor, look at his uniform!"

"I am looking at his uniform, Father," replied Eleanor, without any particular enthusiasm. "That darn on the right sleeve seems to be working loose. I'll mend it after dinner."

"Thank you," I said stiffly. "But I think I'd best get down to the South Meadow to see my men into camp and attend to my letters."

As a matter of fact, there were only two letters, and one of them was a brief note from Barbara wishing me good fortune with Peaceable Sherwood and urging me to capture him as soon as possible — "as Aunt Susanna is so terrified that she has taken to her bed again with the spasms, and we are all in the most melancholy way here." The other letter was addressed to "Colonel Richard Grahame" in a crisp, curiously distinct writing which I had never seen before. It had been sealed with a drop of red wax bearing the impression of a signet ring, equally unfamiliar: a shield, blank except for three little rayed stars in the upper left corner.

> Sir [the letter began politely],
> It gives me infinite pleasure to welcome so distinguished an officer back to Orange County. You may rest assured that I and all my followers will do our utmost to make your stay in this region lively and interesting, though not (I fear) particularly profitable to your Cause.
> With every good wish for your continuing health and welfare, I remain,
> Your very obedient servant to command,
> PEACEABLE DRUMMOND SHERWOOD

I sat regarding this extraordinary communication in helpless silence for an instant, and then put my head in my hands and burst out laughing. I had been right about one thing at least. I was going to have an entertaining antagonist.

It took Peaceable Sherwood exactly one week to

change my ideas of entertainment, and about four to drive me to the edge of raving and insanity. I will spare you the full account of everything that happened. We tried to identify his secret associates — and failed. We tried to unearth his system of communicating with them — and failed again. We tried to track him to his base of operations — and spent six days floundering in the mountains before we finally gave it up. We dispatched spies to worm their way into his organization, and found them tied to the hitching-posts in front of the Presbyterian Church in New Jerusalem the following morning (which was Sunday), with another courteous letter from Peaceable Sherwood, requesting me to send rather more intelligent ones in the future.

I think my men gradually became almost fond of him, as I had known hunters to become almost fond of a certain fox too clever to be caught. To tell the truth, I could very easily have become almost fond of him myself — the man's wit, audacity, and nerve were really admirable . . . if only . . . Oh, if only so much had not depended on the outcome! If only the stakes we were playing for had not been quite so appallingly high! I had once rather liked the notion that I had to save the whole cause of independence singlehanded. Now, I woke up at night in a cold sweat whenever I dreamed of it.

And with every week that went by, Peaceable Sherwood's marauders grew stronger, his raids bolder, his mastery of the situation more complete and terrifying. By August, the whole district was reduced to a state of panic, with frantic citizens hooting at me and my soldiers on the road, and every rider from headquarters bringing dispatches to demand immediate and successful action. The only comfort was that the forest fire Peaceable Sherwood had kindled did not yet spread very far. The British authorities were still making no effort to set up similar organizations in other parts of the country — but this was a poor, thin consolation at best, for surely it could not possibly be long now before they started to do so.

It was the first time in my life that I had tasted real failure or shame, and I found them both uncommonly hard to swallow. In my black desperation, I could not endure the faintest suggestion of help or sympathy from anybody. I even disliked riding over to New Jerusalem because the look in Barbara's eyes was becoming more than I could bear. But such was my perversity that I disliked the look in Eleanor Shipley's eyes even more. Eleanor Shipley, needless to say, was making no effort to burden me with help or sympathy over Peaceable Sherwood. Indeed, there were times when I wondered which of them would really be responsible if I put a bullet through my head.

I did my best to remain very formal, very distant, very courteous whenever I was compelled to speak

to her; and never by the flicker of an eyelash did I
let her know she was hurting me in the least. But
the more formal, distant, and courteous I became,
the more outrageously she conducted herself. I will
spare you the full account of that, also — except to
say that by the end of those ten abominable weeks,
I think I would have cheerfully sold myself to the
devil if he would only have allowed me to trap Peaceable Sherwood by some brilliant maneuver of my
own, and made sure that a certain young lady was
somewhere about to discover when it was too late
how wrong she had been to jeer at Richard Grahame.

"And then she'd be sorry," I muttered fiercely to
myself, as I rode home to my dinner one weary
August afternoon. I was feeling so wretched that
the very thought of food made me sick, but anything
was better than having Eleanor Shipley tell me that
even dashing young heroes needed to keep up their
strength.

It was a blazing day, too, miserably hot and dusty,
without even the promise of a thunderstorm to
break the monotony. All the birds had retreated
into the deep woods, and there was nobody on the
road but a peddler who had taken off his pack and
was resting under the shade of a tree.

Peddlers were becoming rare now that the country was so unsettled, and I reined in my horse to
speak to him on the chance he might have heard

some news. He was one of those slim, lean Irishmen who look as if they were made out of a carriage whip. He told me that he was traveling up the valley with needles and laces and pins and various other gewgaws for the farmers' wives, and asked me to buy one of his ribbons "for my young lady." As I did not feel like explaining just why I had no young lady, I put the question aside and asked him in return if he had seen any sign of Peaceable Sherwood or his marauders on the road.

"May the saints forbid," said the peddler, with a quick glance over one shoulder. "It's ruined I'd be if they caught up with me. Maybe a hunter with woodcraft could slip easy into this terrible great forest and lie snug till they'd gone by. But what would I do that was born in Dublin and me hardly able to tell the woods from the trees, as the old saying has it? Look at that there, now —" waving his hand at a white triangular gash in the bark just above his head. "No doubt a gentleman bred to this land like Your Honor could tell what it means, but sure it might be the blessed Latin itself for all I can make of it."

"We call it a blaze hereabouts," I explained kindly. "Somebody has been cutting it on the tree to mark a trail into the woods. Not a very good man with an axe, either: see where it caught a bit off his clothes? No, over there, hanging on the end of that sliver — by the sumac."

"Sure, and I thought it was a flower, the fine color of it. It's Your Honor has the eyes," said the peddler, reaching for the little scrap and passing it up to me. "A shame to murder the good cloth so cruel. Now if I were back across the water in Scotland before the dreary wars I'd say that was the piece of a tartan."

I nodded as I turned the scrap over my finger to examine it in the light. The wearing of the tartan had of course been forbidden on Scottish soil since the last great rebellion of the clans in '45; but many of the Highlanders who had fled to the New World afterwards had brought their plaids with them — I had one myself which I found useful in the woods when I was hunting. And my grandfather, old Enos, had taught me to know the various tartans and clan badges as strictly as if he were still at home in his hills. "Drummond," I said almost without thinking, as I looked down at the bold pattern of scarlets and yellows and whites.

Then, from somewhere out of the past, I heard the echo of my own voice speaking to General Washington: "The 'Drummond' sounds more as if she might be Scottish, sir."

Perhaps Peaceable Drummond Sherwood also had an old family plaid which he found useful in the woods.

Or perhaps I was simply making a fool of myself?

Yet there was nobody else named Drummond in

this part of the country. Most of the settlers had been Dutch. Piet Cornelius and Joos Van Ghent owned all the land on both sides of the road for miles around.

Yet surely Peaceable Drummond Sherwood would never have been so careless as to catch his fine plaid by accident with the edge of an axe?

But suppose — and I caught my breath hard at the very thought of it — suppose the scrap of tartan had not been caught there by accident? Suppose it had been left on purpose? To mark a particular trail into the woods for someone else to follow?

Yet surely Peaceable Drummond Sherwood would never have marked his trail with a scrap of tartan that might as well have had his name written on it for anybody with the eyes to see.

But who except myself would have had the eyes to see? A thousand other riders might have gone by that tree without realizing the significance of the little rag caught on the sliver any more than the peddler had. Peaceable Sherwood could mark his own gate with his own name, and leave it there quite safely for the public to look at. It was, now I came to think of it, exactly the sort of joke that might appeal to him.

"A fair journey to Your Honor," the voice of the peddler interrupted me. He had risen to his feet, and was yawning and stretching and feeling about for the buckles of his pack. "The road will get no cooler for our sitting beside it, and I want to be over the hills by night. You're sure you wouldn't like to buy a fine ribbon for your young lady, now? Red would adorn her if she's dark like yourself."

"No — her hair is yellow, just like coppery gold," I answered absent-mindedly before I could check myself.

"Have a nice bit of blue, then," said the peddler winningly.

In the end I bought the blue ribbon to get rid of him, and he went away whistling a little tune. He had hardly disappeared around the first bend before I was off my horse to look at the blaze on the tree more closely. As I had thought, the trail was a fresh one. The splinters were still sharp and new, the cut in the bark still almost white. "Probably this morning; certainly not before yesterday," I muttered to myself as I slipped into the wood and on to the next blazed tree like a shadow. Peaceable Sherwood, if it was indeed he, had not made much of an effort to cover his tracks. There was even a path of sorts beaten through the fallen leaves and low bushes.

The path came to an abrupt end at a clearing perhaps a hundred feet in from the road. It was only a little place, all flat mossy rocks with ferns and a whispering thread of water that fell into a tiny pool where —

I took one abrupt step forward and stood looking down at it, while once again the hope died out of my heart.

I *had* made a fool of myself. All my speculations about Peaceable Sherwood and the scrap of tartan must simply have been vaporing. For the little clearing in the woods was obviously nothing but a "secret place" where a child had been coming to play. Barbara and I had once had a "secret place" in our own woods and built ourselves a hut there.

Here there was an old doll crumpled up on a natural seat among the rocks, and a wooden ball lying under a pine farther up the slope. But what had first caught my eye was a sort of toy landscape down by the brook, where the rocks widened to leave a circle of mossy grass. A hole filled with water had been dug in the center for a lake, and moss and pebbles and pine sprigs were heaped about it to represent hills and rocks and trees.

The child, whoever he was, must have worked hard. The little landscape was beautifully made, with a miniature peninsula at one side of the lake, and the hills rounded so naturally that for a moment I had a curious feeling that I was actually gazing at a real landscape from somewhere high in the air. The only thing that spoiled the effect was a withering maple leaf which had been laid, for no apparent reason, over the bare ground where the hills came together at the edge of the water, exactly as they did at Duck's Head Lake.

Then I understood suddenly why the landscape had seemed so real. The child must have modeled it after seeing the view from the big cliff down over the hills and forest to Duck's Head Lake. The peninsula on the right and the rock rising from the water on the left were just the same as those which actually did make Duck's Head Lake look from the cliff extraordinarily like the head of a duck, with the rock for an eye and the peninsula making a bill wide open to quack.

But how could a child still young enough to be playing with toys have ever seen Duck's Head Lake? It was up the mountain, at least four hours' journey away, even for a grown and wood-wise man, in the very heart of the forest. Only hunters had ever gone there, and since the war even the hunters must have stopped coming. It was too dangerous in the present state of the country, when any such lonely place might be the lurking hole of marauders like Peaceable Sherwood or —

Like Peaceable Sherwood?

Peaceable Sherwood and that scrap of tartan which I had thought must be meant to mark a trail for someone to follow.

A trail for someone to follow.

Follow where?

I looked from the scrap of tartan to the toy landscape, my mind working feverishly. Once again my
eye was caught by that singular maple leaf lying so
awkwardly at the edge of the little lake. There was
no reason why it should be there. Had it simply
blown down off a tree? Or — ?

I stooped and picked it up.

Underneath, someone had packed the ground
with water into a smooth square of mud, and then
while the mud was still wet, had stamped it with a
signet ring as if it were the seal of a letter. The mud
had dried hard and the impression was still perfect
— a shield, blank except for three little rayed stars
in the upper left corner.

I sat down on the nearest ledge of rock and began
to laugh almost hysterically out of sheer triumph
and relief. I knew what must have happened now.
Everything was becoming clear to me.

I went on sitting on the rock and worked it all out
step by step. The scrap of tartan was a signal. A
man who had been told to watch for it could slip
quietly off the road as he passed and make his way
up the blazed trail to the little clearing. There he
would find what was actually an excellent relief map
showing him that he was to go on to Duck's Head
Lake. The mark of the signet ring in the mud indicated the exact spot where he was to look for Peaceable Sherwood.

And how beautifully simple the whole thing was!

No letters that might be captured or stolen; no word-of-mouth messages that might be garbled or forgotten. Nothing that could possibly arouse a shadow of suspicion. Who else would have seen anything amiss with that scrap of tartan? And even if he did, it would only be to find, as I had, that he had stumbled on nothing but a perfectly innocent plaything constructed by some lonely child. That old doll crumpled up among the rocks was enough to touch the hardest heart.

Meanwhile, just how many men had come and gone and received their directions since yesterday or this morning? Not, I thought, very many. One or two, maybe; but ten or even five, no matter how cautious they were, would have left more marks in the woods than I had found — and I did not think from the look of the trail that anyone was trying to be excessively cautious. Perhaps they had not yet all arrived, or perhaps this was some special meeting arranged for only one or two chosen lieutenants. Perhaps — O glory! O possibility! — I was still ahead of the whole field, and if I just got to the rendezvous at Duck's Head Lake quickly enough, Peaceable Sherwood would be waiting there alone.

I came to my feet and out of the clearing in one passionate rush, remembering somehow to kick the toy landscape to pieces with my boot as I went by. The scrap of tartan was already in my pocket, and I paused when I had mounted my horse to pull a trail of wild grapevine down over the blaze on the tree. It did not matter how many men came looking for it now: they would have no way of finding out where to go. At most, there would be only one or two with Peaceable Sherwood at Duck's Head Lake; and a chance — more than a fair chance — that there would be nobody at all, and I could have him entirely to myself at last.

The voice of common sense still kept making itself heard fretfully from time to time above the clatter of my horse's hoofs as I pelted up the mountain road as fast as I could go. It went whining on in a nagging way that I could not be absolutely certain of taking Peaceable Sherwood singlehanded, especially if he had even one or two followers with him. And it was imperative to take Peaceable Sherwood; without him his whole organization would fall apart like beads when the string is pulled out. What I ought to do was return to the Shipley Farm first and come back with ten or fifteen men of my own in order to make sure.

But the Shipley Farm was a good five miles in the opposite direction — by the time I got there and rounded up my reinforcements and returned, Peaceable Sherwood would probably either have finished his business or else become tired of waiting and escaped me again. Besides, if there was any more delay I could not hope to reach Duck's Head Lake much before night, and I did not want to go thrash-

ing through a strange forest with fifteen rangers
looking for Peaceable Sherwood in the dark. Fifteen
rangers would undoubtedly make too much noise
even in broad daylight. It was actually wiser to take
care of the whole matter myself. I was a better
tracker than anyone else in the company, except
possibly Lieutenant Felton — and Lieutenant Felton was sickening at the moment with a touch of
malaria; it would really not be fair to drag him out
for such a long expedition on such a stifling afternoon. Anyway, I was going to take Peaceable Sherwood singlehanded if it killed me; and that was the
end of the question. I would no longer put up with
being harried and defeated and mocked as I had
been that summer. I wanted to ride triumphantly
back to the Shipley Farm with Peaceable Sherwood
tied to my stirrup, and find Eleanor Shipley standing at the gate again to watch me come in.

By this time I was well up the mountain, where
the road turned first into a rough trail and then pet-
ered out altogether. My horse had begun to stumble
with weariness too, and I patted him apologetically
when I dismounted to cut through the rest of the
forest on foot.

"Cheer up, old boy, we'll both be famous in the
morning," I said, as I saw to his needs before I left
him. "People will be pulling hairs out of your tail
to remember us by."

Once afoot in the forest, the going was slower,

especially as I had only been in the region twice before on hunting trips, and did not remember the landmarks very clearly. I had also been rather foolish not to go back to the Shipley Farm for my moccasins and hunting shirt. My riding boots were hot and uncomfortable for walking, and my buff-and-blue uniform would have made a fine target for any marauder who happened to catch sight of me among the trees. My sword kept getting in my way too; and it was my only weapon.

Mercifully, however, there seemed to be nobody abroad in the forest. By using every ounce of woodcraft I possessed, I managed to make fair speed. All the same, it was almost evening by the time I came through the last of the pine trees and out under the great rock fall where the hills came together at the edge of Duck's Head Lake. The sun was going down in the west all crimson and gold, and the clear waters of the lake rippled with dissolving colors that melted into dark greens and blacks under the shadow of the towering rocks.

Standing on the highest rock, apparently watching the sunset, was a figure in a scarlet uniform, exactly where the signet on the toy landscape had indicated that he would be.

It was the first time I had ever seen him, and for a moment I could hardly bring myself to believe that he was really Peaceable Sherwood at all. He looked so different from anything I had imagined. He was very slender and extremely young — even younger than I was — with blue eyes and a gentle, curiously calm expression. He stood leaning against a ledge of the rock with an air of careless elegance, as if it were the back of a drawing-room chair, and gazing dreamily down at the dissolving colors in the sunlit water.

Then a twig snapped under my foot as I took an incautious step forward, and I saw him look up.

"That you, Timothy?" he said, without so much as turning his head. He had a lazy, rather drawling voice, and spoke as if it were almost too great an effort to bother.

I came out from under the shelter of the pines, and stood squarely across the only place where it was possible to clamber down from the rock. "It isn't Timothy," I answered.

Peaceable Sherwood stiffened and for an instant seemed to become absolutely still. But when he spoke again his voice sounded only mildly surprised, like a gentleman receiving an unexpected visit from some casual acquaintance.

"Colonel Grahame, I believe?" he inquired courteously. "Won't you come up? Be careful of your riding boots — that rock's slippery. I sometimes think that if I belonged to this country, I would much prefer moccasins and a hunting shirt for work in the woods. As it is, I have to live night and day in this confoundedly uncomfortable uniform to prevent the public from hanging me as a spy when you catch me. Do come up."

Rather taken aback by all this cordiality, I went scrambling across the rocks to him, with a wary eye out for some possible trap or ambush. Peaceable Sherwood merely laughed and shook his head.

"No, I didn't bring anyone with me," he assured me. "There are times when I find the company of even very superior outlaws like my own a little tedious. I fancy all those endless ballads about Robin Hood and his merry men under the greenwood shaws must have been written by virtuous citizens who never even went out of the house. They should have seen old Timothy sitting under a maple tree and eating trout with his fingers. By the way, I hope that nothing is amiss with old Timothy? He had a rather important engagement to meet me here with some other lads in an hour or so."

"We didn't capture him, if that's what you mean," I told him. "He's probably still just trying to find out where you are. I took that scrap of Drummond tartan off the tree, and kicked apart your landscape map in the clearing."

For some mysterious reason, we seemed to be talking together as easily as if we had known one another all our lives.

Peaceable nodded. "So you noticed the Drummond tartan?" he said a little ruefully. "I should have remembered your name was Grahame before I went ruining my auld mither's plaid in that shocking manner. I daresay you were raised on that sort of thing from the cradle, so to speak. Still, I feel the idea was basically a sound one, and that child's playground with the little landscapes has really been useful to me for a long time. Now I suppose I'll have to think of something else."

"That will be quite unnecessary," I said firmly. "You are coming with me."

Peaceable Sherwood did not seem startled or alarmed in the least. The look he gave me was simply one of polite question.

"Am I?" he said. "Now just how are you proposing to go about that, I wonder?" He sounded as if he were only vaguely interested in the problem. "I observe that you are not carrying a pistol, and this rock is really quite unsuited to swordplay. Surely you don't mean to overcome me with your bare hands? I detest wrestling matches."

"That's regrettable," I answered politely, and reached for him.

It was like taking hold of a flash of lightning. Peaceable Sherwood met my attack with one crashing blow that shuddered up my whole arm and almost sent me off my feet; and then I was down by the edge of the rock fighting for my life against a murderous fury that seemed to be made entirely of whipcord and steel. For one precarious instant we struggled desperately; then I felt the heel of my boot slide on the treacherous slippery rock — there was a whirling rush — and I went hurtling through the air into a crashing greenness of pine boughs that closed over me and went black.

When I came to myself again, it was still fairly dark and the light of a full moon was flickering through the branches above me. Someone had thoughtfully removed my coat and rolled it up to make a rough pillow for my head. But when I tottered uncertainly to my feet, Peaceable Sherwood was no longer standing on the rock, and there was not even the rustle of a leaf in the forest to show which way he had gone.

It must have been almost four o'clock in the morning when I finally got back to the Shipley Farm. Somewhere a sleepy cock was beginning to crow, and all the eastern horizon was luminously green with the coming dawn. But it was still black night under the great elm trees by the porch as I let myself into the shadowy hall and went blundering towards my room in the dark.

"Dick?" said a whispering voice somewhere above my head. "Dick, is that you?"

Eleanor Shipley was coming down the wide stairway carrying a lighted candle in one hand. The glow shone on the butterfly blue of her dress, and her white throat, and the coppery glints in her hair.

"Why are you up?" I whispered back. I was so

weary that my voice seemed to come from a long way off, as if it belonged to somebody else. I reached uncertainly for the newel post at the foot of the stairs and steadied myself on it. "Why are you up? Is Felton worse?"

"No, but I expected you back this afternoon, and when you didn't come and didn't come, I thought — Why, Dick!" She broke off sharply and leaned over the banister with a sudden exclamation to look down at me. "Dick, what is it? Are you hurt? Where have you been all this time? You look like death. What's the matter with you?"

I went on standing there stupidly, looking straight ahead of me, not at her, but at the little flame of the candle she was carrying. My voice when I answered her still sounded as if it was coming from a long way off. It seemed to be speaking quietly and dispassionately about another person I neither knew very well nor liked very much.

"I have been behaving like the arrogant fool that I am," the voice said. "I found out by chance today that Peaceable Sherwood was going to Duck's Head Lake to meet some of his followers. I followed him there alone instead of coming back here first to get some help. I told myself that I couldn't spare the time, and the rangers might blunder, and Felton was sick. I was only making excuses for my own pride and folly and spite. I wanted to take him singlehanded as if I were a prince in a fairy tale, and have you looking up to me at last and telling me what a wonder you thought I was."

The voice paused an instant, on a sort of painful breath, and then went on again, even more carefully than before.

"We fought, and my foot slipped because I was wearing my riding boots, like a fool, and he knocked me off the rocks and got clean away because there wasn't anyone else there to stop him. Now I don't suppose we ever will catch him. And General Washington said that I had been recommended to him as an officer with the intelligence and ability needed to carry out a very important mission. Intelligence and ability — isn't that amusing?" I turned my head a little to look up at her. "I see now why you've found me so laughable all these years."

Eleanor was not laughing. To my astonishment, her face had suddenly become a sort of blazing white, and she was so angry that there were actually tears of rage in her eyes. I had not seen her look like that since she was ten years old and flying like a fury at Johnny Tatlock for bullying a small boy much younger than he was. She reached out her hand and caught me hard by the shoulder.

"You stop!" she said, stamping her foot. "You *stop* talking about yourself that way! I won't have it! I won't have it, do you hear me?"

"But Eleanor —" I stammered, almost as completely taken aback as Johnny Tatlock had been in his time.

"Be quiet!" said Eleanor fiercely. "I suppose you think you know more about your own intelligence and ability than General Washington does? Never catch Peaceable Sherwood, indeed! Of all the nonsense! Who almost caught him only tonight? You *would* probably have caught him if your boot only hadn't slipped on the rock, and who cares about a silly old boot? It was all my fault, anyway."

"*Your* fault?" I was beginning to feel that my plunge from the rock must really have unsettled my wits.

"For driving you crazy with my pestering, the way I have!" cried Eleanor. "I knew it was wrong, and I shouldn't have done it, but you never would pay any attention to me, and you were always so formal and distant and courteous, and I was only trying to show you —"

"Show me what, exactly?"

"Oh be quiet!" said Eleanor again, two furious tears spilling over her lashes and falling hotly on my hand. "You always treated me like that, even when you were a boy. You know you did."

"But I thought you didn't like me," I said numbly. "You were always laughing and trying to catch me out and making fun of me. You know you were."

"At least you might admit it was you who began it."

69

"I never did any such thing. I tell you I thought you didn't like me."

"*Like* you!" Eleanor wailed. "I did everything but stand on my head trying to make you take the smallest notice of me! I know I kept talking about your arrogance and your stupidity and your airs, but all the time I would have followed you to China at the hint of a kindness. And when I saw you riding down the road on your horse this spring, I thought you the most —"

It was at that moment I began to laugh.

"Eleanor, I warn you that if you call me a dashing young hero just once more, I shall probably fell you to the earth."

Eleanor began to laugh too, and we both stood there idiotically with our hands linked over the banister, laughing at one another. Then, still laughing, she suddenly bent down to me, and for an instant I felt the mocking mouth brush across my cheek as lightly as a butterfly's wing. The next instant she had pulled her hand out of mine and was running away up the stairs.

The second Richard Grahame sat looking out at the garden for a moment, apparently lost in some pleasant memory. Then he turned his head and smiled at me.

"I told you it was a sad story," he said, "but at least it has a happy ending, and incidentally teaches a useful moral lesson which should prove of great value to your future career."

I felt myself coloring a little guiltily. "If you're thinking about Pat —" I began.

"Well, as a matter of fact, I was," said Richard Grahame. "You were planning to 'show' him something, I believe? Because you have your pride? I thought so. Do let me assure you from my own personal experience that it is a most unsatisfactory method of attracting attention."

"It's only that I haven't heard from him at all," I defended myself. "I don't even know where he is."

"I expect you'll find out all in good time," said Richard Grahame offhandedly.

"Maybe he's just sick of us," I suggested rather dolefully. "I can't understand why Uncle Enos won't make friends with him or even utter a word about him."

"I expect you'll find that out all in good time, too." He had risen to his feet and was moving away towards the other end of the library where the shadows were so thick I could barely distinguish him.

"Wait — oh, please wait!" I begged him. "Just tell me one more thing. *Did* you ever catch Peaceable Sherwood?"

This time there was no answer.

The Cipher Letter

Uncle Enos, who was Peaceable Sherwood?" I inquired the next morning at breakfast.

Uncle Enos, torn from his coffee and the latest issue of *Antiques and Collectors,* merely glowered at me in a blighting manner, and demanded gruffly where I had heard of Peaceable Sherwood.

"Oh, around," I said airily. "I only wanted to know whether he really ever did get caught in the end. They couldn't have hanged him the way they did poor Major André, could they? Because if he was wearing his uniform — "

"I would rather not discuss the subject," remarked Uncle Enos, and started to read *Antiques and Collectors* again.

"But I only want to know — "

Uncle Enos quite deliberately rose to his feet, poured himself another cup of coffee, and made off with the cup in the direction of his study.

I sat there looking after him and thinking how I should love — how *much* I should love — to throw my poached egg squarely at the back of his neck.

Then I remembered that I had never finished looking through the bottom drawer of the Chippendale cabinet, and the answer I wanted might possibly be there. Richard Grahame had saved the scrap of Drummond tartan; perhaps he had kept other things as well.

He had, I found, kept a great many other things. In fact, he apparently had been one of those people who have a sort of mania for collecting souvenirs. There was a faded green ribbon of the kind worn by aides-de-camp in the Continental Army — an eagle's feather — a rough sketch of a four-legged animal labeled MY HORSE GAWAINE — a hunting knife — two pairs of spurs, one broken — an old copy book full of Latin sentences with the words "You must exercise greater diligence" written across the cover in a different hand — a tattered piece of flag that looked as if it might have been picked up on a battlefield — and a little note which read crisply: "Eat what I've left on the hob for you the minute you get in. You won't catch Peaceable Sherwood any sooner by starving yourself to death. — E. S." But there seemed to be no other papers in the drawer, and nothing else that had any connection with Peaceable Sherwood at all. I was just about to close the cabinet again when I caught sight of the letter. It had somehow worked its way between the pages of the Latin copy book, and at first glance I had missed it altogether.

It was only a half sheet of very thin paper, and had once evidently been folded very small as well. The handwriting that covered it was very small too, ancient and faded, but with something still rather jaunty and engaging about the sweep of the letters and the flourish of the capitals:

> better Meet every evening making Us elegant rich music At invitation, letting loathsome Bald aged tyrants Rock For furious ignorant violence, exaggeratedly concerned about Raid pricking their utmost respectability, each wailing as sees humiliation issuing On new glories to Supply our new Train.

I read it through hastily and then went back and read it once more, with an increasing sense of confusion. There was a certain deceptive rhythm about the sentences that carried you along for a moment; they almost seemed to mean something until you started wondering exactly what it was. Why were the loathsome bald aged tyrants rocking? Who was making the elegant rich music at invitation? Each wailing as he sees humiliation issuing on new glories — I was beginning to feel slightly dizzy. I tried again. It would have been easier, I thought, if the writer had not sprinkled his capital letters about quite so eccentrically.

"Oh, not eccentrically," said a voice from the

other side of the room. "Rather carefully, I assure you."

There by the fireplace, beside the deep armchair where Richard Grahame had been sitting the afternoon before, stood a tiny and liltingly pretty girl in a wide-skirted dress of blue dimity, with a glint of ribbon among the curls of her coppery-gold hair. I could see at once why Richard Grahame had compared her to a butterfly — not that she looked at all silly or featherheaded, like the girls who are always being described as "society butterflies" in old-fashioned romances; but she moved with a kind of winging delicacy, and when she dropped down on the big footstool by the armchair, it was really more like alighting than sitting.

"So Dick kept the letter, did he?" she asked. She had a lovely voice, with a sort of mocking caress in it whenever she said the word "Dick," and she put one hand on the arm of the big chair almost as if she were laying it affectionately over another hand that rested there. "I thought he had. Dick always loved to collect things — it was like living in the same house with a jackdaw. He had an untidy little hoard in his desk even at the Farm, when he was almost out of his mind about Peaceable Sherwood and things were at their very worst that awful autumn."

"You mean the autumn just after he lost Peaceable Sherwood at Duck's Head Lake? But I thought

you and he — I mean, you'd made friends with him again, hadn't you? I thought surely it must have been much happier for you both after that?"

It *was* much happier (said Eleanor Shipley); it was so much happier that there were times when I felt as if I'd wakened up out of a nightmare. I could have sung with happiness from dawn to dusk if there hadn't been anything else to worry about. No, it was Peaceable Sherwood who caused all the trouble. Nothing had changed as far as he was concerned — that is, if you could call what was going on "nothing."

Only a week after Dick almost caught him at Duck's Head Lake, he broke out again and destroyed a whole week's supply of grain for the army that was coming down from Kingston. And a week later he burned the powder mill at Iron Forge. Then it was the outpost on the road to Smith's Clove — he had a horse shot under him in the fighting at Smith's Clove, but he contrived somehow to jump clear and got away again. It was almost as if he were protected by some sort of magic. Nothing seemed to touch him. The wildest rumors concerning his powers had begun to circulate among the country folk, and one day even hardheaded old Sergeant Lee begged me for one of my spoons to make a silver bullet. He said it was well known in his part of the country that only a silver bullet would stop a spell-caster.

"Well, why not?" asked Dick rather bitterly,

when I told him about it. "The good Lord knows we've tried everything else."

He was standing with me on the porch for a moment while he waited for his horse. As he turned his head to glance impatiently at the stable yard, I could see how shockingly thin and haggard his face had become under its tan. He had been driving himself hard all summer, but ever since that evening at Duck's Head Lake he had been neither to hold nor to bind. It was as if he could never forget that it was his fault that Peaceable Sherwood was still at large, and every grain of corn he stole in Orange County could now be laid directly to Dick's own act of arrogance and folly. He did not speak of it. I had never heard him mention the matter again after that first morning in the hall. But he was on the road all day and half the night; and if he ever got more than two hours' sleep at a stretch, I can only say that he showed no signs of it. And as for his meals — it was nothing but bread and cheese eaten in the saddle for weeks on end, or soup on the hearth at midnight when I was there to see that he drank it. When he was not out riding the roads, or answering alarms, or following up anything that looked like even the slightest clue, or trying to hold the frantic neighborhood steady, he was at his desk working over plans and reports and maps. Hours after everyone else in the house had gone to bed I could hear him walking up and down and up and down and up and down in the room below.

"You're killing yourself," I told him furiously.

"Well, why not?" asked Dick again. "I can't have very much more time left, and I might as well use it while I've still got it. They'll throw me out of the command any day now, and then I can have a nice long rest while I'm waiting to be court-martialed."

"General Washington isn't going to throw you out of the command."

"What else can he do? The situation can't go on as it is much longer. I expect that delegations from the county trot down to headquarters every week with petitions for my removal signed by hundreds of disgusted citizens. If he'd only let me have more men, I might be able to smash Peaceable by mere brute force or at least scare his secret Tory playmates into staying home and behaving themselves. But there simply aren't the men to spare. They're all needed at the Hudson River forts and the county regiments were cut to pieces on the Minisink this summer. I've written to ask, but it'll be three days at least before I can hear, and even then I know what the answer's going to be."

The three days dragged wearily by, and then became four, and then five, and finally six. On the morning of the sixth Dick rode over to Goshen with some county officials about the signal-fire system, and I went on an errand to a neighboring farm and did not get back till almost noon. As I passed the camp in the South Meadow, I noticed an unusual amount of activity going on — more fires were being built; men were bustling about with forage and blankets, talking excitedly; and scores of dusty horses led by unfamiliar rangers were milling around by the pond as they waited their turn for the water. Wondering, with a sudden lift of my heart, if General Washington really had sent the reinforcements at last, I stopped one of the strangers as he went by the gate and asked him the question.

"Yes, miss, we're rangers too, same company, but I don't know whether we're going to be stopping on here or not. Colonel Van Spurter could tell you — he's up at the house."

Colonel Van Spurter? I wondered as I went on down the drive and up the steps of the front porch. Dick had said that General Washington had once thought of giving the command to an Ogden Van Spurter at the beginning of the whole trouble. Perhaps — but oh, surely not! surely not! It would be too cruel after the way Dick had worked, and the disgrace he was feeling already, and his pride — It was not even as if Colonel Van Spurter were an officer of any sense or capacity. I could still hear Dick's voice saying ruefully only the night before: "If it just doesn't have to be Sputters! You might as well put Peaceable Sherwood in the charge of the village idiot and be done with it."

Colonel Van Spurter, to do him justice, did not

really look very much like the village idiot, but he did most unmistakably look like a large, heavy young man with a great sense of his own importance. I found him alone in the dining parlor by the sideboard, calmly helping himself to an apple from a dish of fruit I had put there that morning on the chance that Dick might remember to eat something in passing. He was gazing around him as he munched with the air of a man who was expecting to stay a long time and was wondering whether the beds and the cooking were likely to prove tolerable. He seemed, on the whole, rather pleased with the furniture and the apple and the view from the window. When I came forward and introduced myself, he was kind enough to seem rather pleased with me, too.

"Well, well, well, so this is Miss Shipley!" he said, waggishly. "I can see now why Dick Grahame hasn't been in any particular hurry to finish his business in these parts. The gay dog! You could always trust old Dick Grahame to find himself the tightest house and the prettiest petticoat anywhere on the day's march."

"That's very good of you," I murmured civilly. "Please don't hesitate to help yourself to that bunch of grapes just because I've come into the room."

"Well, I don't mind if I do," said the gallant colonel, winking at me over the bunch of grapes with his mouth full. "I can see you're one of those girls who really knows how to take good care of a man — eh?" He sucked a grape rather noisily and spat out the seeds into the hollow of his hand.

It was perhaps just as well that Dick opened the door of the dining parlor at that moment and came quickly into the room, his gloves and riding whip still in his hand. His face was quite calm and entirely courteous — but it was the distant, formal courtesy he always drew on like armor when he had to deal with people he disliked. If he had gone to the gallows, I am sure he would have faced the executioner with exactly that air of remote politeness.

"Ah, there you are, sir," he said levelly, closing the door behind him and putting his gloves and whip down on the table. "One of your men was good enough to tell me you were here. What wind's blown you to Orange County?"

"Well, we're just by way of being a sort of advance guard for General Washington," replied Colonel Van Spurter, baring his teeth in what I suppose he meant to be a subtle smile. "He's on the road behind us now with about ten men and a couple of aides — ought to get in sometime before night. The truth is he seems to think the situation around here has gotten so out of hand he ought to come up and find out what's going on for himself. He isn't in a specially good humor, either. You'd better think up a good story to tell him, Dickie old boy. Otherwise, he's likely to fling you out of your command, and appoint somebody who really knows Peaceable Sherwood."

"Ogden Van Spurter, for instance?" Dick's voice was still perfectly level, but I could see the hand that hung down at his side suddenly clench so hard that the knuckles turned white.

"It's possible. You know I never was one to go around blowing my own horn like other officers I could mention, but — well, it's possible."

Dick did not answer, and there was a pause while Colonel Van Spurter finished his grapes, and emptied the handful of rinds and seeds back into the fruit dish on the sideboard.

"What's all this about your having trouble with Peaceable Sherwood, anyway, Dick?" he demanded complainingly. "I'm not one to go around blowing my own horn, but I don't think it would take me more'n a couple of weeks to deal with him, even if I had my hands tied behind my back. Why, I met him myself in New York last winter, and he's nothing to frighten a rabbit — skinny white-faced runt who minces about like a dancing master — most of the time he looks half asleep."

"He must be very different from you, Colonel Van Spurter," I could not help remarking in the sweet, humble manner I used only when I was feeling my deadliest. Dick would have taken warning from the tone at once, but it passed completely over the head of Colonel Van Spurter, who evidently thought that I had fallen victim to his charm, and returned my look with one so warm that it might have ripened the apples in the fruit dish.

"Well now, I guess that's so," he admitted handsomely. "I was never one to go around blowing my own horn, as I say, but — "

"Just how were you thinking of dealing with Peaceable Sherwood, sir?" Dick cut in before he could blow his own horn any more.

Colonel Van Spurter, preening himself a little, offered us three plans in quick succession: two, Dick had tried already, and one so far-fetched that after a slight argument even he was obliged to admit it was impossible.

"Well, what are you doing that's any better?" he inquired at last, rather sulkily.

"Very little, I'm afraid. But I've just gotten on the trail of two farmers in the neighborhood I strongly suspect are secret members of the gang, and my men are watching them now."

"*Watching* them? Why haven't you sent over a squad and arrested them?"

"Partly because there isn't any real evidence yet," Dick explained patiently; "but mostly because I want to find out exactly how Peaceable Sherwood is managing to communicate with them. That's the one weak point of his whole system. He has to send his orders to every man separately, because nobody except himself knows who all the others are. You

84

see why he does it, of course. In that way, he's protected and so are they — anybody taken prisoner won't betray his companions because he can't do it even if he wanted to. Why, we once caught a couple of them who had been riding on the same raids for weeks without ever finding out that at home they were acquainted and even lived across the road from one another! He really is a wonder, that man. But fifty or more separate messages are fifty or more separate chances of something going astray. That's what I'm counting on at the moment. He got around the problem once by working out the most ingenious scheme of setting up an innocent little toy landscape where any number of people could come and consult it. But fortunately we stumbled on that particular trick last August. He's thought of something else since then, no doubt, but he's had to do it in a hurry — and the new method may not be quite so clever or foolproof as the other one. He won't risk making the new method too much like the other one, either, not now we're on our guard. He's probably gone back to some device for sending his instructions to every man separately. It seems to me that our best chance now is to intercept one of those messages, and then before he hears that anything is wrong — "

"Stark nonsense!" Colonel Van Spurter interrupted impatiently. "Nothing will ever come of that; you're simply wasting time. I've listened to some fool plans in my life, Dick, but of all the fool plans I ever listened to, this one is indisputably — "

"Where is he? Where's Colonel Grahame?"

We heard an answering voice shout something from the porch. The next instant there was an excited flurry of feet in the hall outside, and a panting young man dressed like a cowhand suddenly flung open the door and burst without further ceremony into the room. Colonel Van Spurter, cut short in the middle of his tirade, arose magnificently to confront him.

"What do you mean by breaking in on an officer in such a manner?" he demanded, in a voice that would have been more appropriate on the drill ground. "If this is an example of the sort of discipline you keep here, Dick, then all I can say is — "

"Allow me," Dick interposed gently, "to present to you my old friend Lieutenant Charles Featherstone from West Point, who has graciously been spending a few days of his leave working at Jasper Twill's barn in the interests of his country. Well, Charles, what's happened?"

"It came," gasped Lieutenant Featherstone, too full of his tidings to pause or even to glance at Colonel Van Spurter. "It came last night. We've got him now, old boy — got him hooked, gaffed, and put away in the basket!"

"Him? It? Just a little more slowly and coherently, Charles, if you don't mind."

"Peaceable Sherwood, of course! I was mending a harness up in the stable loft this morning, when I saw old Jasper sneaking out into the yard just below me, with his face over his shoulder to make sure nobody was following him. That didn't seem much like old Jasper's usual manner, which tends more to be bold and rude, as a poor wretched cowhand like myself can tell you. And so I drew back out of sight and saw him prying a little sheet of paper from behind a loose rock in that stone wall that runs along there by the road in front of the stables. Then I remembered I'd heard a horse going by the house late the night before, and while of course I couldn't swear that Peaceable Sherwood had been riding the horse, it did seem like a good idea to drop on the back of Jasper's dirty neck and persuade him to let me have a look at his love letter. I've got it somewhere about me now." Fumbling at the pocket of his shabby breeches, he produced a folded note and laid it on the table before Dick, who stood there staring down at it as if he were almost unable to believe in so much sudden good fortune.

"You're sure it's genuine, Charles?" he asked hesitatingly. "Peaceable may be trying to give us a false lead."

"I don't think so, old boy. I've had no chance to really look at it, but it seems to be in some sort of cipher — and besides, Jasper tried to eat it when he saw I'd caught him for good and all. He wouldn't have done that if he'd been told to let me have it."

"Where's Jasper now?"

"Tied up in your South Meadow. I didn't quite know what to do with the other farmhand and that housekeeper of his, but they don't seem to be concerned in this, so I told them to keep their mouths shut and took the liberty of sending over a couple of your rangers to discourage them if they try to leave or talk to anybody. And now *please* may I get out of these abominable clothes and go fishing?"

Dick held out his hand to him with a look of gratitude that made Lieutenant Featherstone blush.

"Charles," he said, "you literally are a blessing in disguise, and I hope you catch a whale."

"Well, just so it's anything but a cow," said Lieutenant Featherstone, saluting us formally and then making for the door. "I never want to see or smell another cow again as long as I live. When I think of the way I used to drink milk as a child, it makes me positively ill."

The door swung shut again behind Lieutenant Featherstone's filthy back, and the rest of us came crowding up around the table to look at the cipher letter. I was so excited that for a moment I could hardly even read the words on the paper as I stood peering down at it under the cover of Dick's elbow: "Better Meet every evening making Us elegant rich music At invitation, letting loathsome **Bald aged tyrants —**"

"Oh, merciful heaven!" Dick's voice was saying ruefully. "It is a cipher, sure enough."

"What's the difference?" demanded Colonel Van Spurter. "I suppose this man Twill can be forced to tell you the key."

"If Peaceable Sherwood's men could be forced to tell anything, Sputters, they wouldn't be in his gang at all. I'm afraid we'll have to struggle on by ourselves. It can't be a very difficult cipher — that's one good thing. Old Jasper's too simple-minded to understand a complicated one."

"It looks complicated enough to me," I said, finishing the letter and beginning to read through it again. "The words as they stand now don't seem to make any real sense — and why has he written so many of them with capital letters? Look, Dick! There's 'meet,' 'us,' 'at,' and — wait a moment! Dick! Doesn't that sound as if it might be — "

"Good Lord, so it does! Go on, Eleanor — all the words with the capital letters. Never mind the rest. They'll be put in simply to fill up space and create confusion."

" 'Meet — us — ,' " I read, " 'at — Bald — Rock — for — ' "

" 'Raid — on — supply — train,' " finished Colonel Van Spurter, triumphantly. "What supply train would that be, Dick?"

"There's only one on the road just now, moving up the Central Valley with gunpowder for West

Point," said Dick, turning the cipher letter over restlessly in his hand and looking down at it again. "But I thought — " he added rather slowly, "I thought that was too much for even Peaceable to tackle. Charles told me they were sending a whole armed guard down to meet it."

"All the better — he'll have to come with every man he can lay his hands on, and we'll haul in the whole gang at one swoop. I've got about fifty rangers of my own with me that I can add to yours — and with eighty in all, it ought to be easy."

"Yes," said Dick, thoughtfully. "Almost too easy."

"And by the way, Dick," Colonel Van Spurter swept on without heeding him, "I think I'd better be the one to command the expedition. After all, I'm bringing more men to it than you are; and even your men were originally in my company to begin with."

"Certainly you may command the expedition, Sputters — if we go."

"What do you mean, *if* we go?"

"Just what I say. I can't explain very well, but . . . I simply don't like the looks of this message, Sputters. It's all wrong, somehow. Can't you see for yourself? It's not like Peaceable. As I said a moment ago, it's — it's *too* easy."

"You mean it might be some sort of trap? But didn't your friend Lieutenant Featherstone say he thought it was a perfectly real message?"

"Yes, he said that."

"Then what in tunket are you worrying about? Suppose it is easy! Peaceable Sherwood would have to make it easy anyway, wouldn't he, if this Jasper Twill is as simple-minded as you say he is?"

"Simple-minded, yes — but not *this* simple-minded."

"Now you see here, Dick!" Colonel Van Spurter stepped back from the table with the air of a man putting an end to all further discussion. "I can't waste any more of my good time sitting around here fretting over what's simple-minded and what isn't. Are you coming, or aren't you? If you're frightened, say so, and I'll take all the men and go by myself."

"You can unfortunately do what you like with your own men, Colonel Van Spurter. But I want it clearly understood here and now that not one of mine is going to stir on any such expedition."

"Permit me to remind you, Colonel Grahame, that I am your superior officer — or will be the moment General Washington sets foot in this house."

"But until that moment comes, sir, you are *not* my superior officer, and have no right whatever to give orders either to me or to any troops General Washington may have put in my charge."

Colonel Van Spurter may have been a fool, but at least he was not the sort of fool who does not know when he is defeated. Snatching up his hat and cloak, he strode quivering with rage across the room to the door, and turned to pause dramatically on the threshold.

"Two hours ago, you'd have been lucky to escape from this business without losing your command, Dick," he said, between his teeth. "Now, you'll be lucky if you escape from it without getting shot for your cowardice."

"Shut the door as you go out," said Dick wearily.

The door slammed, and Colonel Van Spurter's voice was raised in the hall outside, issuing orders that gradually died away in a trampling of feet and clatter of horses' hoofs. Then from the distant camp in the South Meadow there stole up on the drowsy afternoon air a sudden murmur of activity, so faint that it could hardly have been heard by any ears less accustomed to it than mine. Colonel Van Spurter's fifty men had mounted and were riding out by the lower meadow-gate.

Dick paid no attention whatever. He was sitting at the table with his head in his hands, studying the cipher letter again. I watched him in silence for a moment, and then rose quietly to go away and leave him to himself. As I paused on my way to the kitchen to clear away the litter which Colonel Van Spurter had left in the fruit dish, he looked up at me and said suddenly, "Do you think I was right, Eleanor?"

"Of course you were right!" I retorted scornfully. "And only a fool who didn't know Peaceable Sherwood could have supposed you weren't right for an instant."

"I'm not so certain, Eleanor. Perhaps I've been fighting with Peaceable for so long now that I'm beginning to jump at my own shadow. After all, it may be Sputters who's right — we all agreed it had to be a very simple cipher, and —"

I put down the fruit dish on the sideboard once more. My hands were suddenly beginning to shake and I was afraid I might drop it. "Say that again!" I interrupted him sharply.

"What? You mean about its having to be a very simple —"

"But that's just it!" I cried. "Oh, Dick, can't you see that's exactly the reason? Look! You're Peaceable Sherwood. You have to send an important message in cipher to a loyal but not very intelligent member of your gang. You can't make it too hard, or he won't understand it. At the same time, you're afraid of making it too easy because there's just a chance that it might fall into the wrong hands. So what do you do?" I went to him and caught him by the shoulder, fairly shaking it in my eagerness and excitement. "You put in a blazing great false message along with the real one, on purpose to hit the wrong reader crack in the eye, and send him dashing madly off in the wrong direction without looking any further. Dick, I don't want to go around blowing my own horn, as Colonel Van Spurter would probably say, but I think we've got it at last!'

"By heaven, Eleanor, I believe you're right!" Dick put up his own hand and laid it over mine for an instant. "Now let go of my shoulder before you tear it to pieces, and come here and let's see what we can make of all this. It must be something very simple, as I seem to keep repeating over and over again. I presume the real message is hidden somewhere in the other words: the ones we were meant to regard merely as space-fillers."

"And you have to count every third word or so in order to read it?"

"Not the *words,* I'm afraid — there aren't enough of them that would make sense if you tried to fit them into the kind of message this must be. 'Meet' and 'evening' might do, and perhaps 'invitation' or 'violence' at a pinch; but what about 'elegant rich music' and 'utmost respectability' and all the rest of them? No, I think that the real message must be made up somehow out of the letters that form the words themselves. Wait a moment while I get a sheet of paper and some ink . . . Now, taking first things first, I will begin by writing down the first letter of every word if you will read them off for me."

"B," I read obediently. "M – E – E – M – U – E – R – M – A – I – L – L – B – A. That doesn't sound very promising, does it?"

"It does not. Suppose we proceed to the second letter of every word."

"E – E – V – V – A – S – L —"

"Never mind the second letters. Let's try the third."

We tried the thirds and the fourths, and the fifths, and even the sixths, before we were convinced that success did not lie in that direction.

"Very well, then," said Dick, in a determinedly cheerful voice. "We'll have to try combinations — the first letter of first word, the second letter of the second, and so on. That system seems a little stiff for one of old Jasper's intelligence, but I suppose it might do. After all, Peaceable can probably judge old Jasper's intelligence better than we can."

We worked out every possible combination of letters until our fingers were cramped and our brains dizzy with writing them down. The clock in the hall was solemnly chiming four when we finally lifted our heads to look at each other in despair.

"We're all wrong," I said hopelessly. "It must be something about the words themselves."

"It *can't* be the words, Eleanor. The longer I think about it, the more I feel convinced that we're on the right track — we've just made a mistake somewhere, perhaps a very simple one, if we only had the wits to see it. Try once again before we go on to anything else."

There followed a long silence, while we clawed through the scattered papers and sat poring over our blotted lists with our chins on our hands.

"Eleanor!"

"What is it, Dick?"

"Look at this a moment. It's the list we made out of the first letter in every word: B — M — E — E — M — U — E — R — M — A — I — L — L — B — A. Where did that M come from?"

"It was the first letter of 'meet.' "

"And that U?"

"The first letter of 'us.' "

"And the A there, the one after the M?"

" 'At.' "

"Then that's where we made our mistake. You're supposed to leave out the words with the capital letters — the ones that make up the false message. They're not part of the cipher at all. Do you see what that man has done? The capital letters would instantly draw an enemy's attention to the false message. At the same time, they would serve to jumble and confuse the real message if he were clever or suspicious enough to break through to it as we did. *And* at the same time, they would also act as signposts to warn old Jasper not to pay any attention to them! There's the true Peaceable touch for you! Scratch them out and look what you have: B — E — E — M — E — R — M — I — L — L. And that, my dear Eleanor, seems to me very astonishingly like the two words, 'Beemer Mill.' "

"Beemer Mill?"

"It's that old gristmill on the river road, about six

miles from here, the one that was struck by lightning and burned down ten years ago. You must have seen it, you have to pass it every time you cross the river and come up from — Oh, Lord!"

"What is it, Dick? What's the matter?"

"Eleanor, take that sheet of paper and get down the rest of this as fast as you can. Quick! Never mind BEEMER MILL — we know that already — now then, A — T — F — I — V —"

"AT FIVE," I wrote, reading the words aloud as I put them down, stumbling a little in my haste. "CAPTURE WASHINGTON. Capture Washington! Oh, Dick! Was that what you were afraid of?"

"That," said Dick grimly, "is precisely what I was afraid of. Sputters or one of his men must have talked to somebody in a tavern on their way over here, and the word blew back to Peaceable as usual. I suppose he thinks that if he can present a real live commander-in-chief to those boobies at British headquarters, they'll have to give up and take over his system. And what would become of us anyway, with Washington gone?"

"But, Dick!" I was still a little dazed with the suddenness of it all. "Surely they wouldn't dare! They can't just come out of the woods and kidnap the General as if —"

"Why can't they? Of course you think Peaceable wouldn't dare! That's what he's counting on. And the Beemer Mill is the very place to do it, too. The road bends around there under the mountain just before you get to the ford at the millstream. They'll hide in the ruins of the mill until the General starts crossing the ford, and then make a rush and trap them there in that hollow under the mountain. Nothing simpler. Peaceable will come with every man he has, and the General's got nobody with him but a couple of aides and about ten guards — Sputters told me so himself. What time did that fool say they were due to arrive here?"

"He didn't say exactly — just 'tonight.'"

"Well, if they're coming 'tonight,' then I don't see how they can be passing the Beemer Mill much before six at the earliest. Peaceable's men are supposed to be there at five. It's just after four now — if we hurry the horses a little, we ought to get there in time. Who's on duty in the hall there? You! Tarrington!"

"Yes, sir."

"Order all the men to mount: we're leaving at once."

"Yes, sir."

"Pass the word to the stable for my horse."

"Yes, sir."

"And tell Lieutenant Featherstone he can't go fishing till tomorrow."

"This is the sort of thing that always happens to me," said Lieutenant Featherstone, appearing around the corner of the house before Tarrington could even answer, riding his own horse and leading Dick's by the bridle. "I'm so hardened to it by this time that I got into my uniform and saddled up while I was waiting, just on the chance. Dear, dear, what a fine leave I *am* having, to be sure! What a holiday!"

"You can go fishing tomorrow," said Dick, swinging himself up into his saddle.

"But that's what you always say," complained Lieutenant Featherstone dolefully. "What will you bet I never even bait a hook before I go back to West Point? Sometimes I wonder why I put up with you at all. I haven't had any dinner yet, either."

Dick merely rose in his stirrups and shaded his eyes to look down the drive towards the South Meadow. "Tarrington! Can't you get those men along any faster?" he shouted.

"It was all my fault for forgetting the dinner," I said remorsefully. "Do let me cut you some bread and cheese to go with you. Dick, you haven't had a bite since morning. Please? It won't take a minute."

"A fine sight we'd look flashing after Peaceable Sherwood with a drawn sword in one hand and a slice of bread and cheese in the other! Just put some broth on the hob for us before you go to bed. I don't know when we'll be back; if the luck holds, we'll probably have to spend half the night herding a flock of prisoners up to the Goshen jail."

"You mean *you'll* be herding a flock of prisoners

up to the Goshen jail," said Lieutenant Feather-stone, firmly. "And I don't want any broth on the hob either, nasty stuff, probably made out of a cow. Is there any more of that ham left, Miss Shipley? Or the cake with the currants in it?"

Meanwhile, the news of the excitement had apparently spread through the farm like wildfire. I could see distant figures scurrying about the South Meadow like ants when their hill has been stepped on; the two hired men were lumbering up from the barn, the groom was running down the ladder from the hayloft, and Martha had appeared as if by magic from the kitchen, Susan from the dairy, and Deborah from the linen closet, all talking at once and wiping their hands on their aprons. Even the stable dog, losing his head, came dashing out of the yard and flew around in circles, barking at the top of his voice.

I went down the steps of the porch and put my hand on the neck of Dick's horse for a moment.

"Is it likely to be very dangerous, Dick?" I asked as quietly as I could.

"Well, I don't suppose Peaceable is just going to walk up and say, 'Here I am, boys, and which is the best room in the Goshen jail?'" Dick retorted, cheerfully. "Dear me, how unheroic I sound. I ought to be saying, 'We will conquer or die on the field!' as I give you a stern but tender look and bend down from my saddle to kiss you farewell."

"You're not going to die, and anyway I'm so little that if you try to stoop down from your saddle to me you'll probably overbalance and fall right on your face," I pointed out, doing my best to laugh back at him. "Never mind. You can turn for a moment and flourish your drawn sword as you ride out the gate, and I'll stand here on the porch steps and flutter my handkerchief after you in the most approved manner. Goodbye! Good luck! Don't slip on any more rocks! Lieutenant Featherstone, take good care of him!"

The horses wheeled and were off down the lane in a spurt of pebbles and a sudden clatter of hoofs. I put one hand on the nearest pillar to steady myself and stood there looking after them. But the lane and the two riders and the mounted men waiting for them by the gate all seemed to be swaying dizzily together, and I never did see whether Dick actually flourished the drawn sword or not. Then Martha, who was engaged to Sergeant Tarrington, flung her apron over her head and burst dramatically into tears.

"Oh, Miss Eleanor! Miss Eleanor! Miss Eleanor!" she wailed. "Whatever shall I do? He's gone and left me, and I just know in my heart that he's never going to come back again!"

I felt as if an enormous hand had suddenly closed about my own heart and was squeezing it dry.

"You stop that nonsense at once!" I said to her

fiercely. "Do you want to have us all standing around screeching and caterwauling like idiots? Take that ridiculous apron off your head this minute, and do something! Go make a pie for him if you can't think of anything else. Pumpkin's what he likes, isn't it? At least, you're always slipping little pieces of it to him out at the back door."

"Why, Miss Eleanor, I never!" said Martha, lowering her apron and staring indignantly at me.

"That's more like the spirit. Now! Susan, make all the beds up fresh and see that there's a good fire in the parlor and the hall. The nights are getting cold and the men will be chilled to the bone if they're late. Debbie, leave your darning till tomorrow and go scrape some more lint for bandages — we don't know how many we may need. Jonathan, tell my father when he gets in from town that General Washington's coming, and ask him please to see if there's any of the good sherry still left. Amos, I want three chickens for the pot, and another side of bacon out of the smokehouse. Martha, fetch in some more grapes as soon as you've finished making your pie, and don't sob over the filling like that — do you want it to be all salty with your tears when Sergeant Tarrington eats it? He thinks very highly of your cooking, you know. Did I ever tell you what he once said to me about it? Well, he said . . ."

I talked about Sergeant Tarrington until Martha stopped crying and started giggling and blushing and telling me a long story about the first time he had ever kissed her. I made myself listen carefully to every word of it: anything was better than looking down the road and wondering what might be happening at the Beemer Mill. I baked a fresh currant cake for Lieutenant Featherstone. I set the chickens simmering in their broth on the hob. I started a batch of new bread for breakfast. I helped Debbie scrape the lint. I made sure that nothing was missing or out of place in the medicine chest. And all the while, in spite of everything I could do, I found myself listening for the sound of somebody coming down the road — listening so hard that the faintest rustle outside seemed louder than a voice in the same room with me. But at seven o'clock it was only my father riding in from New Jerusalem. At half past eight it was only the minister stopping by on his way home from a sick call near Stonybrook Ford.

It must have been almost nine when I finally heard again the slow clop of hoofs coming up the lane. I sprang to my feet and ran out to the porch, with all the household crowding behind me. In the distance, little points of light were flickering and moving through the South Meadow, and outlined against them I could just make out three shadowy figures approaching from the gate, one riding and the other two walking on either side of the horse. The one on the horse was drooping awkwardly in the saddle, and seemed to have his left arm tied up in some sort of scarf; but his voice as he called up the lane to us through the darkness had a ring in it which I had not heard for months.

"We won, and don't worry, nobody's really hurt," he said. "Charles and Tarrington here weren't even scratched; and the doctor says I've only cracked my collarbone — he'll be up to set it as soon as he's tended to Lyons and Dykinck. There ought to be a law passed to keep me from chasing Peaceable Sherwood across slippery rocks in my riding b — "

He broke off with a sharp gasp of pain as he came down from the horse, and I went dashing into the house again and up the stairs for hartshorn and bandages. By the time I got back, Dick was lying on the bed in his own room, Martha was weeping noisily again in Sergeant Tarrington's arms, my father was pouring out sherry for everybody, and Lieutenant Featherstone was perched on the window seat devouring an enormous slice of currant cake and answering questions between mouthfuls.

"It was a nice little stream, too, just the place for trout when Dick and his confounded rangers aren't roiling up the water with their great thundering feet," he was complaining as I came through the door. "There was nobody at the ruins yet when we rode up, and I could easily have had a cast or two into the old mill pond before they came; but Dick made us all climb the hill and lie close behind the trees and rocks to take them by surprise while they were busy with the General. They went to cover in the mill, of course, just as he thought they would — came stealing up through the bushes by twos and threes, all in their masks and cloaks, like brigands in a romance, while we sat watching and having bets which one was Peaceable Sherwood. There must have been seventy of them at least."

"Was he there? Did you see him?" my father interrupted.

"I didn't myself, not at the time, but Dick said he could tell without even thinking twice about it — something about the way he stood and leaned against the old mill-wheel while he was waiting for the rest to come up. They all hid in the ruins when they heard the General's party on the road, and then went boiling out like hornets the minute it came around the bend into the ford. The next thing I knew we were tearing down the hill after them, and everybody was fighting like mad in the middle of the water. You never heard such a commotion: the poor trout will never be the same again. It was mostly all fists and rocks and every man for himself, if you see what I mean — not very much firing on either side because it was so hard to aim without hitting your own men in the tangle. The outlaws were almost two to one, of course, but our first big charge down the hill had taken them off their feet, and they were beginning to lose their heads. Peaceable Sherwood might have rallied them if he'd had the chance, but old heroic Dick there had gone straight after him over the bank, and was hanging on like death itself when his boot slipped and they both came down with the most awful crash over the rocks. Then about fifteen of his own men went rushing up — they must think very highly of him — and contrived somehow to throw his body over a loose horse and make clean away with it in all the confusion. But they were just the mountain people — his own particular private guard, so to speak. We got every one of the others, I'm thankful to say. They started to surrender in droves as soon as they lost him."

"You mean Peaceable's *dead?*" I asked, hardly able to believe my ears.

"Oh, no — there wasn't enough of a fall. My guess is it only knocked him out," murmured Dick from the bed. "You can't kill that man, except maybe with a silver bullet, as old Sergeant Lee would say. But I think the situation's in hand now. Even if he gets away, he won't be able to do very much damage without his secret Tories to help and supply him. Now they're gone, the whole organization ought to be pretty well finished."

"What did you do with them?"

"They're on their way to Goshen now, in charge of about twenty rangers and General Washington, himself, no less," replied Lieutenant Featherstone airily. "He said he owed it to Dick, and I was to see him home to his bed the instant he was fit to move. We limped in with the rest of the wounded. Nobody else will be back till the Lord knows when."

"How many others were hurt?"

"None seriously. It all happened too fast and there wasn't enough firing. Lyons has a nasty flesh wound through one arm — some of those mountain men must have been carrying knives — and a big outlaw smashed Dykinck over the head with a sharp rock. The others came out of it with nothing more serious than cuts and bruises, which was something of a miracle, considering how heavily we were outnumbered. General Washington wanted to know where Colonel Van Spurter and his fifty men were." Lieutenant Featherstone smiled happily, as if savoring some pleasant memory. "He seemed very much annoyed with Colonel Van Spurter, and said that he was going to deal with him in the morning. I only hope I'm somewhere about when he hears the news. I wonder where he is now? And what's become of that confounded doctor? I thought I heard his sweet, gentle voice outside the door five minutes ago."

The door opened halfway with a jerk, and the doctor said over his shoulder: "Well, stop scratching then!" as he flounced into the room. He was a wizened, peppery little man who seemed to live in a state of continual irritation. He slammed the door with another exasperated jerk and darted at Dick like a dragonfly.

"Didn't I tell you not to go falling on that shoulder again the last time I patched you up?" he demanded peevishly. "What do you think your bones are made of, anyway — granite? And who's that other tom fool you've got out there in the hall? Worst case of poison ivy I ever saw. Must have spent hours crouching in a nest of it. Said he was watching for outlaws or something and didn't notice. Notice! As if anyone but a born idiot couldn't see it grows all over Bald Rock!"

Lieutenant Featherstone on the window seat behind me suddenly uttered a sort of strangled yelp, and Dick sat up in the bed so quickly that he jarred his broken collarbone and gasped.

"Yes, and it's going to hurt you even worse in a minute," snapped the doctor, untying the scarf around the injured shoulder. "Lieutenant Featherhead or whatever you call yourself, come here and hold that candle for me. Eleanor, what are you standing there for? I detest women breathing down the back of my neck. If you must make yourself useful, go away and mix up some slippery elm poultice for your afflicted friend in the hall. And tell him I said to stop scratching!"

I spent a most trying half hour with the disconsolate Colonel Van Spurter, and when I finally got him off to bed and came back downstairs, everything was over and Lieutenant Featherstone and the doctor were out by the hall fire planning a fishing trip and sharing one of the pumpkin pies Martha had made that afternoon. Fortunately, the other pumpkin pie had disappeared out at the back door with Martha and Sergeant Tarrington some time before.

"He'll do now," said the doctor briefly, jerking his head at the closed door across the hall. "Give him some of that hot broth when you settle him for the night — it may help him drop off. Looks half starved to me, anyway. Don't you ever feed him?"

Dick was lying back against the pillows with his eyes shut, very white and exhausted, his left arm in a sling and the free one hanging limply down the side of the coverlet. He seemed only half conscious, and I slipped my own arm under his head to steady him as I fed him the broth. He managed to drink it, and when I put the empty cup down on the night table by the bed, he turned his head a little to look at me.

"Eleanor?" he said drowsily.

"Yes, Dick?"

"General Washington says he's withdrawing the special forces from the County."

"Yes, Dick."

"But he says he'd like me to stay on here for a while with about ten men to get Peaceable if I can, and make sure he doesn't try to start something else."

"Yes, Dick."

"Would you mind very much if I stayed on?"

"No, Dick."

"I don't want to be a nuisance to you."

"Of course not. Hadn't you better try to go to sleep now?"

There was a moment's silence, and I thought he might be dropping off at last. Then the dark head stirred restlessly on my arm again.

"Eleanor?"

"Yes, Dick."

"Do you remember the way we used to fight when we were children?"

"Yes, Dick."

"I scrubbed your face with mud once."

"So you did."

"For telling me what I was thinking."

"Yes, Dick."

"How did you always manage to get even the words right?"

"I don't know, Dick."

There was another silence, so long that this time I thought he must really have gone to sleep.

"Eleanor?"

"Yes, Dick."

"You haven't done that to me for a long while."

"No, Dick, I haven't."

"Could you still do it?"

"I might."

"Can you tell me what I'm thinking now?"

"I suppose so."

"Even the words?"

I drew the dark head over to my shoulder, and put my lips against his hair. "I love you with all my heart," I said to him. "Now will you please go to sleep?"

Eleanor Shipley broke off, cocking her head as if she were listening to something, and then suddenly rose from the big footstool by the armchair.

"I have to go," she said, smiling at me. "That will be Petunia coming down the hall with the mail now."

"But it doesn't matter — it really doesn't matter," I entreated her. "There won't be anything for me anyway."

"How do you know?" She smiled at me again, and then with one of her quick butterfly movements, she was across the room and out through the French window into the garden just as Petunia opened the door from the hall.

"Was that you talking, Miss Peggy?" she asked. "I didn't know where you'd got to since breakfast. This here letter come for you this morning in the mail."

The letter was addressed to me with a very thick pencil in large, uncertain capitals that staggered drunkenly all over the envelope. It looked as if it had been done by a small child who was just beginning school and had not yet grasped the principles of punctuation. The sheet inside was covered with more of the same writing.

"Am stuck fast here Mrs. Dykemann's," it began abruptly:

> Betsy tried to jump fence probably her idea of a joke Betsy unhurt but cracked my collarbone also concussion they wouldn't let me have a pencil till today no further trace of ancestor yet but Mrs. Dykemann has dug up family relic most curious specimen of cipher supposed to have been used by Tory guerrillas during Revolution have made copy to show you if you will just come see me you'll never guess what it is will you please come see me?
>
> PAT

I sat there on the floor by the open drawer of the Chippendale cabinet holding the letter while all the birds in the garden outside seemed with one accord to burst suddenly into song. It was quite a long while before I finally got to my feet and went over to the big secretary to work out my answer.

"Dear Pat," I wrote slowly:

> I worry in lighthouses like cannonballs Can over methods; every association soothes some other opening, So never assert such positive outrageous Guess: see secret inner balance Look lions everywhere Here.
>
> PEGGY

112

The Bean Pot

"PEGGY!"

"Yes, Uncle Enos," I murmured dutifully but not enthusiastically. It was a warm afternoon, and I was very comfortably stretched out in the cool library after a long horseback ride over to New Jerusalem to call on Pat at Mrs. Dykemann's. Mrs. Dykemann, all of a flutter, had given us iced tea on the side porch, with thin watercress sandwiches and a superlative currant cake which she said had come down in her family from the time Eleanor Shipley gave the recipe to her great-great-great-grandmother. "Her name was Martha," Mrs. Dykemann had remarked, "and the recipe was a present from Miss Shipley when she went away to get married, after the Revolution."

"You never told me that, Mrs. Dykemann," Pat reproached her from the hammock. His arm was still in a sling, and Mrs. Dykemann was keeping a careful eye on him.

"The fact is, I'd forgotten it till this minute," she said apologetically. "I guess it was meeting Miss

Grahame put me in mind of it again. Let me see, didn't Eleanor Shipley marry one of the Grahame boys? I know there was some sort of connection. I think Martha worked for her out at the Shipley Farm before she moved to Rest-and-be-thankful. Maybe you've heard about it?"

As I could not very well tell them exactly how I had heard about it, I merely smiled and shook my head and asked for another slice of the —

"Peggy!"

"Yes, Uncle Enos? I beg your pardon. I wasn't attending."

"I've been looking for you," said Uncle Enos peevishly. "Why aren't you ever around when I want you?" That, incidentally, was a fine remark, coming from him. "Where have you been all day?"

"I went for a ride."

"Oh?" said Uncle Enos, losing interest. The question had been intended simply as a reproof. "It's this article I'm writing on eighteenth-century drinking customs for the next issue of *Antiques and Collectors*," he explained, brushing away the whole subject of the ride with a wave of his hand. "I want you to run downstairs for me at once, and see just how many bottles those racks in the wine cellar can hold. I've mislaid my note of the exact number, and I never like going down those steep steps myself: it's bad for my rheumatism."

"Can't you send Petunia?" I asked lazily. I had

ridden almost fourteen miles out and back since morning, and the wine cellar seemed a long way off.

"Petunia! I shouldn't trust Petunia to count six bottles of ginger ale; she's too flighty. You can take her with you to hold the light if you want to. It's dark down there."

The wine cellar at Rest-and-be-thankful was enormous, built in the days when sherry and claret and port and Madeira and brandy appeared every night on a gentleman's table as a matter of course. Uncle Enos himself never drank anything except a modest cup of hot cocoa at his desk before he went to bed, but he took a certain pride in keeping up all the family traditions, and so the sherry and claret and port and Madeira and brandy were still there in their long dusty racks, as if waiting forlornly for the jolly old butlers and the liveried menservants who never came any more. It was very dark indeed, and the stairs were even steeper than Uncle Enos had led me to suppose. Cobwebs touched our faces at every step, and unseen creatures ran before our feet with unpleasant scampering noises. It seemed a long time before I finished my count, and then I had to do it all over again, because Petunia was so frightened by the darkness and the rustlings that she kept putting me off by giving sudden squeaks of terror and wavering the light with her unsteady hand.

"Eighty-seven — eighty-eight — *will* you keep

still, Petunia? Eighty-nine — if you drop that candle, we'll probably have to stay here all night — ninety — ninety-one. No, we are not going to run back to the stairs. I want to look around a little. It's an interesting place."

And since at the bottom of my heart I was actually feeling just as uncomfortable as she was, I took particular pains to saunter slowly and casually back to the door, looking idly about me and asking questions, as if I were mildly curious and not especially anxious to leave.

"What do you keep in there, Petunia?" I inquired, making myself pause almost at the cellar steps to point to a queer sort of door, lurking sullenly in a corner, half concealed by the angle of the stairs. It was made of iron grating, like the door of a prison cell, and was fastened on the outside, top and bottom, not only with two long rusty bolts but a clumsy large lock as well.

"I don't know, Miss Peggy!" protested Petunia, trying unobtrusively to work me on up the steps. "You won't find nothing in there. Mr. Enos says it ain't been open since the Revolution."

I went over to the door and tried to lift the upper bolt, which fell with a deep grinding moan. Petunia gave another squeak of terror, and almost dropped the candle again.

"Haunted!" she said in a sepulchral whisper. "Don't you go in there, Miss Peggy."

116

"Nonsense, Petunia. See! There's nothing in here but cobwebs and maybe a few — ouch!" I had stumbled and nearly fallen over a rounded object half buried in the dust on the floor. It appeared to be a jar of some sort, but had become so caked and encrusted over the years that it was almost unrecognizable. As I straightened up again I felt a touch on my shoulder, and peering around, saw that I had brushed against two ugly iron chains suspended from the wall. I could not understand why they had been hung there until I caught sight of an iron ring attached to one of them. They were shackles.

"Come on out of there, Miss Peggy, before something gets you," wailed Petunia unhelpfully, from the doorway.

"All right," I answered rather shakily. "I'm coming."

Uncle Enos was back in his study, a jeweler's glass at his eye, examining two antique wineglasses from the corner cabinet of the dining room. The first Richard Grahame was supposed to have brought them back with him from a voyage to Italy when he was a young man. They were lovely things, fragile as bubbles. One was pale sea-green flecked with gold, the other a blazing crimson that was almost scarlet. There was a plunging dolphin curved about the green stem, and a curling snake twisted around the crimson one, both blown with incredible delicacy out of the glass itself. The rest of the desk was covered with old books and papers and masses of untidy notes.

"Thank you, child," said Uncle Enos with unusual good humor, when I made my report. "I dislike going down to the cellar. What's that thing you've brought up with you? It looks like a small Colonial bean pot."

"I fell over it in that little room with the grated door and the chains on the wall."

"Oh, that one." Uncle Enos was already turning back to his desk. "Old prison," he informed me absent-mindedly, as he leafed through a pile of notes. "First Enos Grahame built it. Used it to scare off Indians. Country still pretty wild around here when he settled. Had a theory they'd never attack the place if they once got the idea it meant being caught and shut up. Never actually put anybody down there as far as I know."

"Then how do you suppose that the bean pot — "

But Uncle Enos was now thoroughly tired of rewarding me for my good behavior. He reached for a small leather-bound book that lay among the litter of papers, and opened it rather as if it were a door through which he was trying to usher me out of the room. "Can't you see I'm busy?" he demanded testily. "Do run along and don't bother me, like a nice child."

I did not feel at all like a nice child as I retreated to the library, and flung myself passionately down in Dick's big armchair by the fireplace. I hated being a nice child. I did not want to be a nice child. I wanted to be a mean, nasty, horrible shrew and go yell in Uncle Enos's ear until he gave up and told me who had left the bean pot in the cellar.

"I overlooked it at the time," replied a matter-of-fact voice from the other side of the room. "Very slatternly of me, I confess, but my thoughts were in a state of some confusion. And of course, we had Captain Sherwood on our hands too, and as Richard said, *he* couldn't be trusted even when he was unconscious."

It was Barbara Grahame again. She had just closed the hall door behind her and was coming forward into the room. She still had on the same long crimson cloak that she wore the first time I met her; and I noticed with a slight feeling of surprise that in spite of the summer heat the hood was pulled up around her throat and knotted there over a little sprig of pine and red berries as if it were a cold day in the Christmas season.

"Tell me, Peggy," she said, with a sudden delightful smile that made her look like her brother, "did you find any beans in that pot?"

"No — only dust. It looked just like plain, ordinary dust to me, too. The pot must have been scraped clean when it was left in the cellar."

"Between Dick and Peaceable, I suppose it was.

Peaceable always did have such an astonishing fondness for baked beans." She laughed softly as if she were remembering something that entertained her. "He used to say that the baked bean was the one poetical food New England had ever produced."

"*Peaceable* did?" I repeated in bewilderment. "But — but when did you ever know Peaceable? He got away with his men after he was hurt at the Beemer Mill, didn't he? I thought you were over at New Jerusalem with your Aunt Susanna all the time."

Indeed I was (said Barbara Grahame), and a weary time it seemed to me, too. Even when I was a baby, there was nothing I hated quite so much as being taken over to call at Aunt Susanna's house. It was one of those little houses, very small and dark and dismal, where you always feel as if it must be raining outside, no matter what kind of day it is. Dick once told me it smelled of misery; though of course it was really only the damp and the medicine. But I believed every word he said (I must have been about six, then), and used to sit on the edge of my chair trying to smell the misery myself, until Aunt Susanna thought I was getting a cold in my head and made me drink some horrible black syrup before I went home! Aunt Susanna terrified me. She had fat white fingers, very soft, but with curiously sharp, horny nails that were apt to scratch as she patted me gently on the cheek; and there was a sort of whining edge in her fat, soft voice that could hurt just as badly as the nails did. No matter how hard I tried, I always flinched and shrank whenever she made me sit on her lap; but it was never any use — Aunt Susanna simply held me down with one remarkably powerful hand, while she looked appealingly at my father and said it was really very sad to be so old and ill and burdensome that even her own little niece couldn't spare a moment out of her happy life to be kind to her poor sick auntie. And then my dear father would feel that he had to talk to me about it very patiently and sweetly all the way home!

It was the same old story again many years later, when she coaxed him into closing Rest-and-be-thankful and sending me to live with her at New Jerusalem while he and Dick were away with the army. I flinched and shrank. Aunt Susanna talked about her loneliness and her sorrows and her ills while she held me down. My father was very patient and sweet with me — and it all ended exactly as I had known it would: unpacking my boxes in the little corner bedroom where, as Aunt Susanna pointed out, "you can easily hear me if I happen to be awake in the night and want company." And with that she told me to fetch another pillow for her head, and settled back against it to enjoy herself.

I remember the months that followed only as a sort of nightmare of carrying trays and measuring out medicine and answering calls and trying to persuade Aunt Susanna that Peaceable Sherwood was very unlikely to burn all New Jerusalem over our heads while we slept. The whole house smelled of misery worse than ever. The cook was exhausted, the kitchen-maid sulky, and the underfed "bound out" boy so unhappy that he seemed always to have a sort of mournful drip at the end of his nose. Dick and Eleanor did their best for me, of course. But they had so many troubles of their own that summer I could hardly ask them to carry mine as well. Aunt Susanna did not care to have me wasting my time on anybody but herself, anyway. She was likely to develop terrible fluttering pains that needed all my attention whenever she heard one of my friends asking for me in the hall downstairs, and a simple invitation to a housewarming in November brought on an attack of the vapors that lasted almost a week. Even when I asked if Dick and Eleanor might not come over to spend the afternoon of Christmas day with me — a request we thought she could not possibly refuse — the words were hardly out of my mouth before she was discovering all sorts of reasons why she could not possibly consent.

"Come over to spend the afternoon with you? A young unprotected girl ride all that distance alone with no other companion than your brother?" cried

Aunt Susanna, as if she were hearing of some hideous scandal. "The very idea!"

"They're going to be married just as soon as Father can get leave to come to the wedding, Aunt Susanna," I ventured to remind her wearily.

"That makes no difference. If Edward Shipley has one spark of proper feeling, he'll keep that daughter of his at home. When I was young, your grandfather would have whipped me soundly and sent me to bed without my dinner for so much as mentioning any such jaunt."

I then suggested that instead I might ride over to the Shipley Farm myself on Christmas morning, and spend the day with Dick and Eleanor there.

Aunt Susanna uttered a little shriek of astonishment and disapproval.

"Ten miles out and ten miles back again on that forsaken road in all this snow — have you gone clean crazy, child?" she demanded indignantly. "Suppose you happened to meet the villain Sherwood?"

"Aunt Susanna, how could I possibly meet the villain Sherwood when he's hiding somewhere up in the hills and hasn't been heard of for months? Dick even thinks he's fled the neighborhood altogether. Won't you let me go — please? Only this once?"

"And leave your poor sick auntie by herself tomorrow of all days of the year, old and lonely and suffering as she is? In my day, young people were satisfied to stay home and take care of their betters. No, don't argue with me, Barbara — you know how the slightest argument harrows up my nerves. Oh dear, oh dear, I feel as if one of my bad headaches is coming on already."

"You'll feel better when I've fetched you your evening gruel, Aunt Susanna," I cut in hastily, and got myself out of the room before I completely lost control of my temper. Stamping into the kitchen, I slammed the porringer down on the tray, and spooned gruel out of the pot with a viciousness that almost sent it flying in all directions over the floor, my head whirling with furious crazy plans to get to the Shipley Farm — somehow — anyhow — and then Aunt Susanna could say what she liked to me when I came back. She had cheated me out of my home and my comfort and my brother's companionship for the past eight months. She was *not* going to cheat me out of Christmas Day with him as well.

Yet even as I stood there raging, I knew in my heart that she not only could, but would. Running away was out of the question. It was impossible to escape from that house — in fact, it was impossible to so much as move from room to room without fatally attracting the attention of Aunt Susanna, who, for all her sixty-five years and her twenty-seven diseases, had the eye of a hawk and the ear of lynx and the persistence of a mosquito. Of course, she had said upstairs that "one of her bad headaches was coming on" — and when she really had those headaches, she always took a drug in the morning that sent her to sleep for the rest of the day. But I put no faith in anything Aunt Susanna had said upstairs. I knew all about the bad headaches and the terrible fluttering pains and the dizzy spells that were always "coming on," only to vanish mysteriously again as soon as she got her own way.

For once, however, Aunt Susanna was apparently telling the truth. I awakened in the dawn with the sound of her shrill voice screaming in my ears, shrieking for her sleeping drops and threatening to die if she did not obtain them immediately.

"Couldn't you get here any faster, you lazy, slow-footed good-for-nothing, you?" she welcomed me politely, as I appeared in the doorway with her spoon and glass in my hand. "Does nobody in this house care if I perish, or did you all intend to go on resting like the dead until the Judgment Day?"

"I'm sorry, Aunt Susanna," I apologized, holding the glass to her lips; "but we had some difficulty making up the dose. You see, the bottle is nearly empty, and — "

"Nearly empty? Do you mean that not one of you had the common intelligence to see that it was kept properly filled? Take yourself to the apothecary's while I'm asleep and buy me more. After all, there's no reason why you should sit about the house idling the whole day because I'm not awake to keep an eye on you."

"I'll go to the apothecary's after breakfast, and I promise you not to sit about the house idling the whole day, Aunt Susanna," I murmured obediently.

Aunt Susanna began another sentence that ended in a snore as I went out of the room, closing the door carefully behind me. I suddenly felt so lighthearted that I almost danced a jig on the doormat, and I broke a little Christmas spray of pine and red berries for my cloak as I stood on the steps waiting for the horse. Even the bound-out boy had begun to whistle faintly when he came up the path from the stable leading the fat mare which Aunt Susanna considered the only safe mount for a lady.

I was just settling into my saddle when I felt a timid touch on my boot, and glancing down, saw that it was the exhausted cook, nervously concealing a small object under her apron.

"You going out, Miss Barbara?" she asked in the beaten, toneless voice all the inmates of Aunt Susanna's house fell into the way of using sooner or later.

"The mistress wants some medicine from the apothecary's, Hannah, and I was planning to go for a ride afterwards. Why? Would you like me to do anything for you?"

"If you're sure you don't mind taking it, Miss Barbara? It's only a piece of my special fruitcake to

126

give Mr. Dick, all wrapped up nice to fit into your pocket. Mr. Dick was saying to me the last time he was here that he would sure relish a taste of my fruitcake this Christmas."

I stared down at the cook with a little gasp, and the cook stared back up at me without a flicker on her jaded, expressionless, overworked face.

"You don't know anything about this, do you, Hannah?" I asked, warningly.

"I ain't even seen you, miss," retorted Hannah, and marched back into her kitchen again.

The fat mare and I ambled together down the road to the apothecary's. We had gone there so often that the apprentice recognized the sound of the hoofbeats, and was smiling on the path to receive me before I could even rein in at the door.

"Merry Christmas, Miss Barbara," he called to me cheerfully. "And what will it be today? Hartshorn? Seneca oil? Peruvian bark?"

"Headache drops," I answered, returning his smile and handing down the bottle. "Will you just ask Mr. Elliot to fill this for Miss Susanna Grahame and then fetch it out to me afterwards, so I needn't dismount? I'm in haste today."

"And so you should be, Miss Barbara, to go by the looks of that sky."

I did not like "the looks of that sky" myself. A pale silver sun, faint as the moon, was doing its best to break through the haze overhead, but along the whole northern horizon the heavy clouds lay dark and threatening, while an icy wind had already begun to crisp the puddles and scurry through the heaps of fallen snow. I studied the clouds rather anxiously as I waited, hoping against hope that the storm would at least hold off till I got out to the Shipley Farm. I had often ridden longer distances than ten miles simply for pleasure, but never in the dead of winter and never on such a broad, stupid, underexercised excuse for a horse.

"Here it is, Miss Barbara," said the apprentice, dashing back out of breath to thrust a small parcel into my hand. "And please, Mr. Elliot says to tell you that the last supply of that drug was much stronger than the ordinary, so you must reduce the dose from four drops to two, and measure with the most particular care. And he does beseech you to be cautious, because seven drops will knock a strong man flat, and any more of it he won't answer for the consequences."

"Tell him I understand. Thank you, Henry, and a happy New Year."

"And to you, miss," said the little apprentice. "And if I may presume — don't lose any time getting on to the house. It's going to snow again."

It *was* going to snow again. The sun was already gone and the sky darkening wickedly when I reached the fringes of the village. There were very few people on the road. The one woman who passed me walked hurriedly, glancing over her shoulder at the clouds and dragging a stumbling child sharply by the hand.

As we went by the last house, the fat mare gave a disgusted snort, exactly like one of Aunt Susanna's, and sensibly tried to swerve back in the direction of her stable. But I set my jaw and ruthlessly thrust her on. I had made up my mind. After all, I was a strong rider and I knew every inch of the way. There were five miles of rather rough, difficult going until one got over the hills and came out down by the Tatlock Farm — then almost a mile past Tatlock's cornfields and meadow and pasture land to Martin's Wood and the left-hand turn there to Rest-and-be-thankful — and finally, four more miles of excellent road winding away up the valley to the Shipley Farm. With any luck, the snow ought not to begin for another hour or so. Once I got in, it was welcome to come down as hard as it liked, preferably hard enough to make it impossible for me to go back to New Jerusalem for at least a week.

Unfortunately, however, the storm chose instead to break suddenly and full blast just as I got over the hills and rode out down by the Tatlock Farm. It came with one tremendous whirling rush of driven ice and razor wind that staggered the fat mare and almost sent me reeling out of my saddle. The next moment we were both floundering desperately in choking snow and screaming gusts. Dazed and half-blinded, I steadied the frantic horse and wildly looked about for the nearest place of shelter.

There was none. The familiar country all around had melted and vanished into a swirling whiteness that was like thick fog. Tatlock's cornfields and meadow and pasture land were all gone as if they had never existed. I knew Tatlock's house lay somewhere across the fields to the right, with Hopegood's a quarter of a mile beyond it, but I dared not even try to start towards either of them — I would be hopelessly lost and very likely dead in a ditch five minutes after I left the road.

Then I thought of going back the way I had come, but going back meant five miles against the storm over slippery rock and dangerous slopes — too great a risk, even if I had had the strength to force my horse directly into the wind. There was nothing to do but press on and trust my luck to reach the Shipley Farm sooner or later. The roads were better in that direction, and the gale would be at our backs. I could rest the fat mare awhile in the cover of Martin's Wood; it was only a mile away.

It was a hideous journey, and it seemed to go on for hours. The wind beat and tore at us incessantly. My hands became so stiff with cold that I could hardly keep hold of the reins. The wild torrents of snow were suffocatingly thick. It was still almost impossible to see — at any moment we might have lurched over a smothered rock or gone off the road altogether. The fat mare stumbled and sobbed.

"Careful! careful down there, old girl!" I tried to encourage her. "And I wish to heaven I'd taken your advice back at New Jerusalem, if that's any satisfaction to you. Can't you get along any faster, you lazy, slow-footed good-for-nothing, as Aunt Susanna would say? We must be fairly near Martin's Wood now."

Martin's Wood was swaying murderously in such a fury of straining trunks and whipping branches that I wondered if I ought to linger there even a moment. But any shelter was better than none, and at least under the trees we were not beaten and overwhelmed by the full force of the gale, as we had been out in the open — it was possible to pause, to breathe, even to see a short distance down the road. I guided the mare to a staggering stop against the bulk of a gigantic oak with a windbreak of young pines behind it, and there we rested wearily, while I tried to gather up the last remnants of my strength and courage to face the long four miles still to follow. But by that time I no longer cared greatly whether we ever got to the Shipley Farm or not. I wanted to go on resting. It was warmer in the woods than it had been in the fields — much warmer — in fact, I felt quite warm and comfortable leaning up against the oak . . . very comfortable . . . only so tired . . . so tired . . . sleepy . . .

I caught myself sharply. I was getting overcome

with the cold. I had been a fool to stop at all. I would have to go on. If I did not go on, I would die.

Numbed and quivering, I gathered up the reins again in my stiffened hands and looked along the highway to find out if the storm was showing any signs of slackening off. It was certainly snowing less heavily than it had been. I could see my way clear to the last of the pines and the lane that branched off just beyond to Rest-and-be-thankful. I could even make out the turn itself, and — I leaned forward unable to believe my eyes — four . . . six . . . no, at least ten dark figures on horseback coming down the road towards the crossing. All the breath of my body seemed to rush to my throat in one sob of relief and thankfulness. There was only one man in the region likely to be out with ten mounted men on a day like this.

I flung up my head, and sent my tired voice down the road as far as it would go.

"Dick!" I called frantically. "Dick!"

There was an answering call from the foremost rider — I saw him turn his horse and the others crowd in behind him — then a hand was steadying my arm, and a gentle voice I did not recognize was asking what had happened to me?

"The storm caught us," I answered weakly, too faint with cold and exhaustion even to look up. "Almost a mile back . . . on my way to Shipley Farm

. . . I'm Barbara Grahame . . . didn't Dick come with you?"

There was a little murmur of surprise from the circle around me. A man laughed and another voice made a remark which I did not catch — a harsh voice, stinging and disagreeable, but this time a voice which I was sure I had heard somewhere before. I tried to glance down at the speaker, but my head was beginning to swim — and all I could see was a mass of dim shadowy forms that kept wavering and dissolving and wavering back again.

"Where's Dick?" I whispered painfully. "Didn't he come with you?"

"No, Miss Grahame. He was still in the house when we left it," the gentle voice answered; "but you'll see him as soon as we can get you there. Put your hand on my shoulder — so. I'm going to take you over on my horse with me. You're too far gone to ride by yourself."

I put my hand out blindly — then there was a dreadful moment of plunging confusion — and then the sharp pressure of an epaulette against my cheek roused me for an instant again to feel a hard arm around me and hear what seemed to be the end of a command: " . . . sure to fetch her mare along with you, Porson."

"Now you listen to me, Capt'in!" It was the harsh voice again, angry and protesting. "Why don't we

133

just take the mare and go? You leave that girl where she is, and never mind none of your hifalutin, fancy gentleman stuff! Somebody else'll find her. Lord ha' mercy! Ain't we got enough trouble?"

"Your lack of proper feeling disappoints me very much, Porson." The gentle voice was exactly as gentle as ever. "Are you by any chance trying to argue with me?"

The last sound I remembered with any distinctness at all was the harsh voice saying "No, sir" submissively. . . .

. . . The gentle voice was speaking somewhere a long way off, urging somebody to wake up and swallow. Somebody swallowed obediently, got a mouthful of hot brandy that made her choke, and opening her eyes, found herself stretched out before a crackling fire on about two armchairs and six pillows, a blanket tucked over her shoulders, and a young man in a black cloak kneeling beside her with a wineglass in his hand.

"Better?" said the young man, swinging to his feet and setting the wineglass down on the mantel. "No, don't try to sit up yet — just lie quietly, while I go see if I can open one of these confounded window blinds. I'd like to lay my hands on the fool who thought fit to design them."

"Where's Dick?" I murmured sleepily.

"All in good time, Miss Grahame," the gentle voice floated back from across the room. "Just lie quietly and rest another moment — though I'm thankful to say there's nothing wrong with you but cold and a little too much exhaustion, which you've been sleeping off nicely by the fire for the last three hours. And that mare of yours is safe in the stable — that is, if Porson hasn't fed her a poisoned carrot by this time. She had the good taste to kick him twice when he was trying to bring her in."

Still only half awake, I lay contentedly listening to the voice and watching the blessed firelight flicker over the andirons and the big footstool and the — I caught my breath with a sudden gasp — the black splotch on the hearth where Christopher had spilt the ink the day we closed the house eight months before.

Very slowly and cautiously I turned my head.

I was not at the Shipley Farm. I was in the library at Rest-and-be-thankful.

The locked secretary — the bookcases draped with sheets — the stack of curtain rods I had thrust into the corner to clear them out of the way — the whole room exactly as I had left it, except for the young man in the black cloak, who had at last contrived to wrench open the inner blinds of the south window, and was standing there gazing dreamily out at the falling snow. He had a thin, very calm, and curiously attractive face, with lazily drooping eyes that made him look almost half asleep.

And at that moment I remembered precisely

where I had once heard the harsh voice that had spoken in Martin's Wood. It belonged to a man named Abraham Porson, an old soldier who had kept the George Tavern on the Goshen road until he disappeared under peculiar circumstances just after the skirmish at the Beemer Mill. General Washington had halted his line of prisoners at the George that night while he and the guards drank a glass of flip to celebrate the victory. By the time they finished the flip and called the proprietor to bring the score, the proprietor had mysteriously vanished, taking two of the General's prisoners with him. Dick later discovered that he was the only member of the gang who by some chance had not received his orders and joined the attack at the Beemer Mill.

I stared aghast at the young man by the window, suddenly and most horridly convinced that I knew exactly who he was and exactly what he was doing there. Dick had always maintained that with his secret Tories gone and his supplies cut off, it would only be a question of time before cold and hunger forced him and his few remaining followers down from their hills like so many starving wolves or catamounts. But that he should dare to take shelter in Rest-and-be-thankful itself — yes, that was quite reasonable too, when I came to think of it. Rest-and-be-thankful was, of course, the last place in Orange

County where Dick would ever dream of searching for him.

The young man at the window glanced up, caught me looking at him, and lifted one shoulder in a slightly rueful shrug. Then, very slowly and deliberately, he removed his cloak, came back across the room with the firelight making one glorious blaze of his scarlet and gold, and stood gazing down at me in silence, a quizzical, faintly amused glint in his sleepy eyes, as if he were waiting for me to shriek or cower or swoon away, like a well-bred girl with the instincts of a lady. Unfortunately, however, as Aunt Susanna often remarked, I entirely lacked the instincts of a lady, and had no intention whatever of shrieking or cowering or swooning away for anyone's entertainment, least of all his.

"I am very grateful to you, Captain Sherwood," I said with calm politeness, "for saving my life."

The quizzical, faintly amused glint disappeared from Peaceable's eyes. He dropped down on the big footstool, where he had a better view of my face, and sat there with his arm across his knee regarding me with a new look — grave and considering — as if he had suddenly found it necessary to form an entirely new opinion of my character.

"And I am grateful to you, Miss Grahame," he answered, "for accepting the situation with so much intelligence. I thought you would go into hysterics when you found out who I was. But do let me assure you that I was well brought up, little though I may look it just now" — he glanced mournfully at a patch on the left elbow of his scarlet coat — "and you really have nothing to be afraid of. I'll see that you get back to the Shipley Farm somehow — as soon as I can."

"Now, that *is* kind of you," I said, smiling at him. "I don't want my poor brother going out of his head worrying over what's become of me."

Peaceable Sherwood picked up the tongs from the rack and bent forward to attend to the fire.

"That need not concern you, Miss Grahame," he replied, in his gentlest voice. "He knows you're here."

"What?"

Peaceable Sherwood did not turn his head. He was very carefully thrusting a blazing stick back under the big log and pulling up another to make the fire burn better. It was almost as if he did not wish to see the look on my face when he answered me.

"Your brother, Miss Grahame, very foolishly rode over alone to this house last night to find some trifle or other he wanted to give Miss Shipley for a Christmas present. He is now locked up in your little private prison at the foot of the cellar stairs."

There was a dead silence. For one terrible moment I thought I was going to scream aloud — everything began to waver and dissolve again — then I got control of myself, and came rigidly upright against the cushions of my chair, with my hands clenched over the arms so hard that I could see the tendons standing out. Then somehow I managed to unclasp the hands, and laid them quietly together in my lap.

"How very fortunate for you, Captain Sherwood." My voice was just as level as his own; I might have been congratulating him on finding a stray shilling.

Peaceable Sherwood straightened up sharply, and sat there regarding me again with that odd, grave, considering look on his face. It was a moment before he replied. When he did, he sounded almost absent-minded, as if his thoughts were really on something else.

"Very fortunate indeed, Miss Grahame. I have found it practically impossible to form a new organization while your brother remains in charge of this district — the neighboring farmers' respect for him appears to be even greater than my own. When they once find out he is safe with us in the mountains, I trust I shall have no further difficulty with them."

"You intend to take Dick back to the mountains with you?"

"Of course, Miss Grahame. This is only a brief

expedition to obtain supplies, you understand. When we return in the morning, your brother will naturally accompany us."

I almost said, "Not if I can prevent it!" to his face; but I bit the words back, and lay there in silence gazing down at him and thinking harder and faster than I had ever thought in my life before. At that moment, it was a little hard to believe that I couldn't get Dick out of his clutches somehow — he looked so young and innocent sitting on the footstool with the fire tongs in his hand that any mother in New Jerusalem would have walked up and given him her baby to mind without an instant's hesitation. Then I remembered the scene in Martin's Wood, and Abraham Porson's insolent voice saying "No, sir" submissively. Abraham Porson had been known as a "hard man" when he kept the George Tavern; it was his favorite boast that no one could force him to change his mind or compel him to obey an order.

"I wouldn't try it if I were you," said Peaceable Sherwood, suddenly.

"Try what?"

"Whatever it is you are going to try," retorted Peaceable, hanging the fire tongs back in their place. "And now would you care to pay a brief visit to Colonel Grahame while they're setting up the table here? I ventured to order Christmas dinner served in the library at half past two, in the hope of having your company."

"May I take Dick a piece of fruitcake the cook gave me for him this morning?"

"Certainly, Miss Grahame."

The fruitcake, wrapped in a damp napkin to keep it fresh, was in the outer pocket of my cloak, just underneath the little sealed bottle which contained Aunt Susanna's headache drops. I dipped my right hand into the pocket and closed it carefully about them both to conceal the bottle as well as I could; then with a quick movement I lifted them out, and transferred the cake boldly to my left hand while I quietly slipped the bottle down a hidden fold in the trailing skirt of my riding habit.

Peaceable Sherwood apparently failed to see the bottle at all. At least, his gentle face did not change by so much as a quiver as he courteously assisted his guest to rise and conducted her through the empty rooms to the cellar door with all the ceremony of a gentleman-in-waiting handing a duchess through the halls of a palace. The cellar door he unlocked with a small key he took from his waistcoat pocket and then put back with a mocking quirk of one eyebrow at me.

"Merry Christmas, Barbara," called my brother from the gloom at the foot of the stairs. "Captain Sherwood told me you were here."

"Merry Christmas, Dick," I called back, feeling my way down the steep steps one by one. "Hannah sent you a piece of fruitcake."

"Good old Hannah!" He accepted the fruitcake through the bars of the door with a brushing kiss on the back of my hand as he took it. "How is she, these days?"

"It desolates me, Colonel Grahame," interrupted a pleasant voice from the open door above, "to remind you that enemy ears will be obliged to listen to every word of your conversation. I regret the necessity for so much caution, which I beg you to believe I should not dream of using if I did not consider your sister a very remarkable young lady." He had seated himself at the topmost step and was leaning lazily against the door frame. I could see his thin profile delicately outlined in shadow on a square of lighted wall halfway up the stairs.

"I only wish you could have met her under more pleasant circumstances," Dick was replying with equal courtesy; "and forgive us if we bore you with all the family news. Have you heard anything of Father lately, Barbara? Or Mr. MacTavish? What's become of dear old Mr. MacTavish?"

I stared at my brother in bewilderment. Mr. Mac-Tavish was a disagreeable fool of an elderly Scotsman, once our tutor, who had, much to our joy, quitted Rest-and-be-thankful in fury ten years before, when my father refused to agree with him that the Iroquois Indians were descended from the Lost Tribes of Israel. I had long since forgotten his very existence.

"Mr. MacTavish, Dick?" I echoed uncertainly. "Why, you know as well as I do that I haven't seen Mr. MacTavish in — "

"And please tell Hannah I was never more hungry for a piece of her fruitcake in my life," Dick cut in loudly before I could complete the sentence. "Not that Captain Sherwood hasn't fed me well, you understand — in fact, he breakfasted with me down here only this morning: we had a most entertaining talk on field-fortification and got through a whole quart of baked beans between us. That's the crock now, rolling about on the floor there by your left foot — your *left foot*, Barbara."

Then I understood. Back in the evil days of Mr. MacTavish, Dick and I had invented a simple method of conducting conversations with our feet under the cover of the schoolroom table. It was an almost foolproof system of little taps and pressures, easy to learn and impossible to forget once you had learned it.

I drew a deep breath, and stealthily moved the toe of one riding boot an inch nearer the door.

"We received a letter from Father only last week, Dick. He's been stationed at Philadelphia for the winter, very comfortably except for the difficulties his friend General Arnold is having with the Congress. Aunt Susanna, thank heaven, continues fairly well, though she complains of dizzy spells, terrible fluttering pains, wakeful nights — " Safely launched on the long list of Aunt Susanna's complaints, which I could reel off by the hour without thought or effort, I cautiously advanced my toe another inch and met Dick's toe under the grating.

" — indigestion, palpitations of the heart . . . KEY. WHERE. QUESTION MARK."

"PEACEABLE. POCKET."

" — spasms, fits of coughing, faintness . . . WILL. GET. KEY."

Dick's boot merely came down heavily across my instep with a dull thud that had once meant, DON'T TRY ANYTHING SILLY, NOW.

" — occasional headaches, shortness of breath, unnatural fever, and nervous attacks."

"Poor Aunt Susanna! Give her my affectionate regards. What's she dosing herself with nowadays? Remember when it used to be vinegar, rhubarb . . . MEN. FEAST. KITCHEN. TONIGHT. . . . laudanum, antimony . . . DRINK. HEADS. OFF . . . sulphur and molasses . . . WON'T. WATCH . . . elixir of rose hips . . . YOU. DODGE. PEACEABLE. GET. AWAY . . . poppy seed and hot lemon juice?"

"She's changed to Seneca oil and Peruvian bark now, with sleeping-drops for her headaches . . . WON'T. LEAVE. YOU."

"FOOL. NITWIT. MUTTONHEAD . . . Sleeping- drops? I thought the war had cut off the supply."

"There must have been another shipment. The apothecary filled an order for me only this morning

144

on my way here. That's how I contrived to get away." I made the sign which had once meant: YOU JUST LET ME HANDLE THIS, WILL YOU?

"NO. EXCLAMATION MARK. REPEAT. NO. DANGE ——." He broke off abruptly with the word half-finished, and gave me the sudden kick in the ankle which had once meant: BE CAREFUL THE TEACHER IS WATCHING US.

"Dinner is served," said Peaceable Sherwood from the top of the stairs, "and little as I like to interrupt this exceedingly interesting conversation, I must ask Miss Grahame to accompany me back to the library."

"Bring me the crusts when it's all over," was Dick's only comment. "And don't let Barbara eat the mince pie if there is any. It always gives her nightmares."

Someone had evidently worked hard in the library during our absence. My tangle of pillows and blankets and armchairs had disappeared, and in its place a small table was drawn up before the fire, and decorated bravely with pine sprays, lighted candles, a strange array of mixed crockery, and an even stranger collection of assorted foods.

"What have we here?" said Peaceable Sherwood, courteously seating me at the head of the table and beginning to uncover the dishes one by one. "Will you object if I wait on you myself, Miss Grahame? — my men, though excellent riders and very fair shots, are rather unskilled in the little niceties of

145

passing the butter and handling the gravy. The chicken and the ham I can recommend. They came from Mrs. Tatlock's oven no later than this noon. The wine you probably know better than I do — at least you ought to — it's your own. Mrs. Hopegood's plum pudding I hesitate to offer you. I distrust the cooking of any woman who faints away at the very sight of a British uniform."

"Have you been robbing the Hopegoods and the Tatlocks?" I demanded indignantly.

"The Hopegoods and the Tatlocks and the Barlows, and the Smiths and the Van Dusers and the Browns, to be exact," replied Peaceable Sherwood complacently. "I daresay they'll all be clamoring for justice down at the Shipley Farm as soon as the weather clears, just like the good old days. Do have a little of this stuffing. Ah! More baked beans! I discovered the baked bean, Miss Grahame, when I was in Boston with General Gage in '76. Why is it that people who can cook such admirable beans seem quite incapable of making a pot of tea that's fit to drink? I never had a really good cup of tea the whole time I was there. No wonder the poor wretched populace finally revolted and threw it into Boston Harbor by the ton! That reminds me — did you ever hear the story about General Gage and the time he tried to talk about the Boston Tea Party to the deaf old lady who thought it must be some sort of social occasion? One of the Loyalist dignitaries was giving a reception for the staff officers, and it seems the old lady — "

The story was so outrageously funny — especially the way the old lady kept repeating, "Very odd to brew the tea with salt water, very odd indeed!" — that I broke out laughing in spite of myself, and simply could not resist telling him in return about the afternoon that old Madam Losser arrived to call on Aunt Susanna with her pet spaniel, and what happened when the spaniel accidentally lapped up some of the medicine in Aunt Susanna's saucer while nobody was looking. And after that — I did not quite know exactly how it happened, but somehow we both seemed to be laughing and talking and having a little more of the chicken, as if we were sitting together over a real Christmas dinner with the fire and the candles making a circle of light and warmth all around us. By the time we came to the nuts and the wine, we were arguing like old friends about Aunt Susanna, Peaceable insisting that he had an uncle of his own who was even more trying to live with than she was.

"And at least she isn't your guardian," he pointed out firmly. "Do reflect for a moment on the horror of having my Uncle Anthony for one's nearest surviving blood relative!"

"Is he really so bad?"

"I may be doing him an injustice. The first time he saw me, twenty-two years ago, he informed me that I was the ugliest little rat of a newborn baby he had ever seen in his life; whereupon I instantly tried to stick my finger in his eye — and so we have gone on ever since. The only consolation is that it's so hard to believe he really exists, and isn't just some figment of a playwright's imagination. He roars and flourishes his cane and stamps his gouty foot exactly like one of those tyrant fathers in a very bad comedy. I never see one of his performances that I don't start looking around for the orange girl and wishing it was time for the curtain to come down. Still, I must admit that, all things considered, I owe him a good deal."

"You mean he actually is like a tyrant father in a comedy, with a heart of gold hidden under his crusty exterior?"

"Oh, no. I was only reflecting that if it had not been for my Uncle Anthony's wretched temper and deplorable lack of self-control, I should not be sitting on the other side of this table enjoying your company at the present moment."

"What?"

"It's very simple. Uncle Anthony was with the army himself in his younger days before the gout felled him, and he's still in a position to make a considerable nuisance of himself at the War Office. He bought me a commission when these troubles broke out, and had me shipped off to America with strict orders that I was to be given the hardest and dirtiest post available — preferably one from which I should never return. Tell me, did you or your brother ever happen to wonder why Sir Henry Clinton was so slow to take up and multiply my little organization for discontented Loyalists?"

"Dick did wonder — often. He thought that possibly Sir Henry was too stupid to understand the merits of the plan."

Peaceable laughed softly and a little bitterly. "Oh, it wasn't that, Miss Grahame. He was perfectly capable of understanding the merits — if it had only been John André or some other officer in good standing who presented the plan. But unfortunately, you see, it was *my* plan — and my uncle has so many friends at court back in England that he'd sooner touch poison."

"But that simply isn't possible! You can't be serious! Surely, if he's your own uncle, he wouldn't — "

"Why wouldn't he? You live seventy years or more in a place where you own every man and woman and blade of grass for a day's ride in any direction, and then see how you behave when you can't make somebody do what you like. He called me an ill-conditioned lout, and an ungrateful young mongrel, and — oh, never mind. The scene went on as it always did, and after a while it ended as it always did, too. He started waving his cane and swearing before God he'd break my cursed stubborn spirit if it killed me, and I started laughing at him and told him he was welcome to try. And so — " concluded Peaceable, dismissing the whole subject with a careless wave of his hand, "he tried."

"But why was he so angry with you? What on earth had you done to him?"

"I wouldn't marry the half-wit he'd selected for me."

"The . . . what?"

"Half-wit. Oh, she didn't bay at the moon," Peaceable admitted grudgingly. "Or gnash her teeth, or think she was a rabbit. Uncle Anthony even gave me to understand that she was very highly regarded in her own circle. But she was the most unutterable *fool!* She used to say 'La, sir!' and giggle, and flutter her fan whenever I spoke to her."

"All the young ladies you meet do that nowadays. It's the fashion."

"Precisely what my uncle said to me. To which I replied that if that was the fashion, I'd rather die single. I intend to get married when I meet a young lady as intelligent as I am — and not before. Miss Grahame, what are you laughing at?"

"I beg your pardon," I choked apologetically. "I know it's rude to laugh, but — b-but it was the way you said it, as if all you had to do was just give her notice of your intentions — a-and I was only wondering how you'd feel if s-she had the — the intelligence to refuse you."

"She won't, Miss Grahame. I'm like my uncle — remarkably set on having my own way. So were all the other Sherwoods, as far back as the family history goes. We even have a motto about it on our coat-of-arms: *Quod desidero obtineo* which roughly translated from the Latin, means: I get what I want."

"You wait until you meet the young lady, Captain Sherwood."

"I met her, Miss Grahame, this afternoon."

He said it quite slowly and casually, without the slightest change in his lazy voice — indeed, he was not so much as looking at me, but twirling the stem of his wineglass absent-mindedly between his fingers and staring dreamily at the fire. Unfortunately, however, I knew Peaceable Sherwood fairly well by that time, and his air of elegant heedlessness did not deceive me in the least.

"You aren't drinking your wine; let me fetch you some from the dining-parlor sideboard — Italian — Father brought it back from Rome," I interrupted him hastily, and ran out of the room before he could say anything else.

I knew it, I knew it, I ought to have made him lock me up with Dick in the cellar, I thought, my heart pounding as I fumbled with the door of the dining-parlor sideboard. Oh, why didn't I stay at home and learn to flutter my fan like a sensible girl? I got down the Venetian glasses from the corner cabinet and filled them carefully with the Italian

151

wine. Then I reached down the hidden fold of my riding habit for the bottle of Aunt Susanna's headache drops, trying to remember exactly what it was that the little apprentice had told me that morning. How many drops had he said it would take to knock a strong man flat?

"Seven," I murmured, breaking the seal on the bottle and turning my head to listen. Across the hall in the library, the tongs clinked faintly as Peaceable Sherwood mended the fire again. Somewhere a long way off in the kitchen I could hear shouting and the sound of feet stamping happily on the floor. A man with a high sweet voice was just beginning to sing a plaintive, wailing little tune. It was the old ballad about the girl who lost her lover by her hardness and her cruelty.

"In Scarlet Town, where I was born,
There was a fair maid dwellin',
Made every youth cry Well-a-Way!
Her name was Barbara Allen.

All in the merry month of May,
When green buds they were swellin' —"

"Get on with it, can't you!" I told myself fiercely. "The longer you put it off, the worse it will hurt in the end. You were a fool to let him talk to you at all."

> *"So slowly, slowly rase she up,*
> *And slowly she came nigh him —"*

the voice from the kitchen sang behind me as I put the glasses on a tray and went back across the hall to the library.

Peaceable Sherwood was still lounging in his chair and gazing down at the fire. He did not glance up when I entered, nor did he try to return to the interrupted conversation about the intelligent young lady. He simply sat there looking most alarmingly like a man prepared to go on sitting there patiently, for years and years, if necessary, until he got what he wanted.

"These are the Venetian glasses," I said rather too quickly and nervously, putting one down on the table before him and returning to my own seat with the other. "Father brought them from Italy especially to serve this particular wine. Mine, you see, is shaped like yours, but sea-green and decorated with a dolphin instead of a snake. Curious, aren't they?"

Peaceable lifted his, and regarded it gravely. It shone in his hand like a jewel. The snake curled around the stem glittered and flickered in the firelight as if it were alive.

"Very curious," he agreed with me placidly. "And so easy to tell apart. No chance of the wrong person getting the wrong glass, is there?"

153

"No, I suppose there isn't. Don't you think we ought to drink a toast? To the New Year? Or the end of the war? Or anything you choose?"

"Certainly, Miss Grahame. And since these are the Venetian glasses, suppose we drink it after the Venetian manner?"

"What is the Venetian manner, Captain Sherwood?"

"This."

He moved so quickly that I did not even realize what had happened until I suddenly found myself staring down at the crimson glass on the table before me, and Peaceable Sherwood back in his chair languidly examining the dolphin curved about the stem of the green one.

"In Venice," he explained kindly, "the host and the guest always exchange their glasses before they drink a toast — I understand the fashion dates from the time of the Renaissance, when one never knew precisely when one might be poisoned. Pretty custom, isn't it? I have a great liking for pretty customs. They add so much to life. " Then, without altering his voice in the least: "What did you put in it, Miss Grahame? Your Aunt Susanna's headache drops?"

"I don't know what you mean," I stammered weakly.

"That's very fortunate, Miss Grahame. I should hate to see anything happen to you. Would you care to propose the toast now, or shall I?"

"Please give me back my own glass, Captain Sherwood, and stop this nonsensical foolery."

"But is it nonsensical?" inquired Peaceable, dreamily. "I wonder."

"Please, Captain Sherwood! I happen to dislike this particular glass very much. I — I have a horror of snakes."

"Indeed, Miss Grahame? I thought of you as a woman with a soul above these trivial superstitions."

"I tell you, Captain Sherwood," I insisted desperately, "that I did not put poison in your wine."

"You discourage me, Miss Grahame. I told your brother an hour ago that you were a very remarkable young lady. Now I begin to think that you must actually be as foolish and as silly as any other member of your silly, foolish sex. Don't you know that it was very stupid of you to think you could remove that bottle from the pocket of your cloak and conceal it in your riding habit without my knowledge? And that it was even more stupid to inform your brother that the apothecary sold you a sleeping drug only this morning on your way here?" He was speaking now very gently and quietly, like a sensible person trying to reason with a — I gulped bitterly over the word — a half-wit. "And do you really suppose that you can sit there and ask me to believe that there is nothing in that wine but wine? I don't blame you for trying, you understand. It's only the general lack of intelligence that annoys me."

"You're wrong," I retorted, but my voice sounded feeble and unconvincing in my own ears. "You're wrong."

"I am delighted to hear it, Miss Grahame — and I beg your pardon for misjudging you." He bowed to me apologetically across the table. (There could unhappily be no doubt that he was enjoying himself very much.) "I assume that we can now proceed to our toast without further discussion? Since I have your word that there is nothing amiss with your wine, you will of course feel no hesitation about drinking it with me."

Or, less politely: take that drug and prove yourself a liar; refuse to take it, and prove yourself a liar just the same.

"I never drink with people who distrust me, Captain Sherwood."

"But in this case may I persuade you to break your rule?" He leaned forward and pushed the crimson snake into my fingers with a grave courtesy that made me long to pitch it at his face. "I propose a toast to my intelligent young lady — if she exists," he added, and emptied his glass.

"To your intelligent young lady, then, Captain Sherwood," I responded calmly — and emptied my own.

Peaceable Sherwood turned sharply, and we sat looking at one another for a long moment in a stillness so tense that I could hear the logs whispering in the fire, and once again, very faint and far off, laughter and voices from the distant kitchen. A whole chorus was singing now. The lilting words came clear and curiously distinct through the silence.

"O when I was a young man, I lived to myself,
  And I worked at the weaver's trade:
And the only, only thing that I ever did wrong
  Was to woo a fair young maid.

  I wooed her in the winter-time,
    And in the summer, too:
  And the only, only thing that I ever did wrong,
    Was to save her from the foggy, foggy dew —"

Peaceable Sherwood drew a long breath and set down his glass carefully in the exact center of his plate.

"The only, only thing that I ever did wrong," he remarked. "It was in the green glass all the time, wasn't it?"

"I didn't know how I could get the bottle out of my cloak without your seeing it," I answered, in a voice that was suddenly rather shaky and exhausted. "So the only chance was to let you see it, because then you might think it was amusing to pretend you hadn't. You like watching other people make fools of themselves, don't you? And leading them on, and outwitting them, and hanging them with their own rope at the very last minute? I told Dick about the sleeping drops in the cellar just to make certain. Anybody else would simply have taken them away from me, or refused to drink anything at all, or spilt the wine by accident — but not you: that wouldn't have been entertaining enough. I was almost sure you'd get the notion of exchanging those glasses, because it was so much more clever. And I shouldn't attempt to rise if I were you, Captain Sherwood. You'll be unconscious in another moment."

But Peaceable had risen already — to this day I do not know how he did it — swaying dizzily, with one hand clenched over the back of his chair, yet insanely, unbelievably, erect and unruffled.

"A gentleman can hardly continue to sit," he explained, in his serenest and most level voice, "when he asks a very remarkable young lady to do him the honor of marrying him. And — " he somehow contrived to grin at me wickedly, "I usually get what I want, Miss Grahame," he added, and pitched over in a tangled heap on the floor.

Then I fear I made a fool of myself. I began to laugh wildly; then I began to cry; then my head was down on my arms and I was sobbing and choking and shaking uncontrollably, in a manner that would have disgraced even the most die-away female who said, "La, sir!" and giggled and fluttered her fan whenever anybody spoke to her. It took a sudden stamping of feet and a wild outbreak of applauding

yells from the kitchen to remind me sharply that I was even yet in no position to sit there luxuriating in my own tears and hysterics. The early December twilight was already closing in; Dick was still in the cellar; we were a long five miles from the Shipley Farm and safety; and at any moment Abraham Porson or one of his drunken companions might take it into his head to wander down the hall and glance into the library as he passed.

Key, my weary brain insisted as I struggled to my feet. Key — Dick said he had it in his pocket, with the other one.

All the house keys were in Peaceable's pocket, fastened together on their ring — Dick must have brought them with him and then lost them when he was taken on the previous night. They clashed noisily in my shaking hand when I pulled them out. I tried frantically to quiet them with the other hand as I ran down the hall past the closed door of the kitchen. But the tipsy voices inside were roaring the chorus of "Foggy, foggy dew" so loud that I might have driven a coach-and-four up the corridor without attracting the slightest attention. The big kitchen key was still standing in the lock where they had left it, and I risked stopping an instant to turn it very softly before I darted on to the cellar. Dick was sitting on the floor beside a candle stuck in the empty bean pot, whistling "The only, only thing that I ever did wrong . . ." in harmony with the music upstairs. He came to his feet as he caught sight of me.

"I put the sleeping drops in his wine," I whispered, fumbling desperately with the locks and the bolts. "The rest of them are shut up in the kitchen. And he said the horses were all down in the stable. Oh, hurry, Dick! What are you standing there for?"

Dick thrust the candle into my hand, and turned his head to glance up the stairs.

"You get down to the stable by the hedge path from the cellar and start saddling up," he whispered back. "I'll be with you in a minute or two. Where's Peaceable?"

"In the library, but — oh, come along, Dick! Please come along! You can't —"

"Do as you're told!" said Dick briefly, and was gone up the stairs.

It must have stopped snowing while we were still having dinner in the library: everything was quiet when I opened the cellar door, and there was a glint of clear sky above the feathery drifts clinging to the tall hedges that lined the path. The stable was warm and shadowy and already dark. I put the candle in a lantern and hung it on a nail before I turned to the horses. Most of them looked thin and shabby and rough-coated, as if they had been having hard times lately. The only ones that seemed to be really in good condition were Dick's charger Gawaine, my own mare, and a sturdy little chestnut cob that had apparently come from the Tatlock Farm along with the chicken and the ham that morning.

"Home you go, boy," I told him, as he pricked his ears and whickered appealingly at me. "This your saddle? Gently, now — gently! I suppose you were led astray by bad company? . . . Well, I must admit it can have a good deal of charm sometimes."

A low voice said, "All well, Barbara?" from the doorway, and I heard Dick's feet on the saddling floor behind me, walking slowly, as if he were carrying a heavy load. I turned quickly, and the light from the lantern caught the white upturned face and the limp arm in the patched scarlet sleeve swinging down over his shoulder.

"Here, come help me with him," he said, panting. "We'll have to put him down across the saddle and tie him on somehow, I suppose. You seem to have done a nice, thorough piece of work while you were about it. He probably won't know he's even on earth till morning. Not that I'd really trust Peaceable anywhere short of a cemetery, and then only with a large, heavy monument to hold him down, if you see what I — Careful! careful! steady, that's right. Now bring me some cord out of the cupboard over there on the left. No, the *left*, you nitwit! Good. Now keep his hand steady a moment so I can get at the wrist."

The thin hand stirred an instant as my own closed around it, and then relaxed helplessly again. "Oh,

Dick!" I said in an uncertain whisper. "Dick, do you have to?"

"Want him sliding off the horse?" grunted Dick, bending down to lash the wrist to the stirrup-leather.

"No, I didn't — it isn't that . . . I mean, do you have to take him with us when we go? Do you *have* to?"

Dick straightened up abruptly and gave me a look of the liveliest exasperation.

"Of course I have to take him with me!" he snapped. "And he'd have to do the same to me if he had the chance. You know that as well as I do. What's the matter with you, Barbara? This is a fine time for you to start behaving like a female, I must say! Women!"

He swung himself up on his own horse with a disgusted snarl, and we filed out of the stable and down the drive in silence. The party in the kitchen had apparently not yet discovered that anything was wrong. The fires and lights were still blazing festively behind the drawn curtains as we passed them, and the man with the high sweet voice had begun to sing "Barbara Allen" again. The last plaintive, reproachful notes floated lingeringly after us on the clear evening air:

> "*O mother, mother, make my bed,*
> *O make it saft and narrow:*
> *My love has died for me to-day,*
> *I'll die for him to-morrow.*"

Then the house fell away behind us again, and there was nothing to be heard but the faint jingle of the harness as the horses turned into the orchard road and quickened their pace a little. A handful of winter sunset was burning fierily on the dark edge of the western hills, the sky above it clear gold and citron deepening slowly to a luminous blue that was already pricked with stars. Dick lifted his head and looked at them.

"Fair day tomorrow," he said thoughtfully. Then, in precisely the same tone, "I'd give ten years of my life to know exactly how this happened."

"I told you," I answered, rather shortly: I did not feel like talking just then. "I put Aunt Susanna's sleeping drops in his wine."

"And I suppose that was all there was to it?" retorted Dick. "I said I wanted to know what happened. You may be a very remarkable young lady, my dear sister, as I seem to remember somebody observing in the cellar, but you'll never make me believe that you just poured Aunt Susanna's sleeping drops into Peaceable Sherwood's cup and he drank them down like a good little boy without any trouble whatever."

"I don't know what you'd call trouble. He asked me to marry him, if that's what you mean."

"Barbara!" said Dick sternly. "Barbara, do you remember what happens to little girls who tell lies?"

"He asked me to marry him."

"Not truth and honor?"

"Truth and honor. He also informed me that he usually got what he wanted."

"He did, did he?" Dick gave a long whistle of amazement and then suddenly began to laugh. "I believe that he's supposed to have made the same remark once before — when he tried a perfectly impossible attack on an army outpost last August. One of his men was telling me about it this morning. He said that Peaceable had no more chance of taking that place than he had of flying away to the moon."

"Did he take it?"

"Oh, yes," said Dick. "I'm sorry for you, Barbara. When's the wedding?"

"I think you are behaving in an extremely rude and ungentlemanly manner," I replied with calm dignity. "And besides, how can there possibly be any wedding when he's under lock and key in the Goshen jail?"

"I expect you'll find that out," said Dick, placidly.

"Peggy!"

I glanced up — it was Uncle Enos again, calling to me from the study — and when I looked back, Barbara Grahame was gone. Only, for an instant, lingering like a cool breath on the heavy summer air, I thought I felt the faintest possible winter tang of Christmas pine and wood smoke. Then a great puff of hot wind came tearing through the east windows and swept it away as the curtains billowed and the study door blew open with a crash. At the same moment the room darkened suddenly and there was an ominous rumbling roar overhead. The long heat of the afternoon was breaking at last in a thunderstorm.

"Peggy! Where are you?"

Uncle Enos was standing at the open window of his study struggling frantically with the catch. Heavy drops of rain were beginning to spatter all around him. Loose papers and notes were blowing in showers about the floor and the Venetian glasses on the blotter rocked and tinkled perilously in another rumbling gust of wind. The small leather-bound book Uncle Enos had been reading that afternoon slipped from the edge of the desk and fell, carrying a stack of manuscript over with it. I sprang forward to catch the glasses — there was a tremendous roar of thunder — and then the window had slammed shut and I was down on my knees trying to gather up the scattered pages of the article Uncle Enos was writing for *Antiques and Collectors*.

Uncle Enos paid no attention to me. He was back at the desk examining the Venetian glasses with trembling hands to make sure they had come to no harm. Mercifully, it was all over so quickly that nothing had really been hurt. The sheets of manuscript were out of order, but none was missing and only two appeared to be even slightly blotted by the rain. The small leatherbound book was lying open face-down on the rug, and for a moment I thought the fall must have split it apart, but when I picked it up and ran my finger along the spine, it did not seem to be damaged at all.

It was a nice little book, very old and smelling faintly of dry paper. Rather to my surprise, there was no title on the spine — not even a few faint traces to show where a title had once been before it was worn away — nothing but a coat of arms stamped in faded gold on the center of the front cover, with a —

"Peggy!"

The book was snatched out of my hand, and Uncle Enos stood over me, glaring down, his lips white and his eyes blazing with fury. I had not seen that look on his face since the appalling afternoon when he had driven Pat out of the house, almost a month before.

"And just what did you think you were doing?" he demanded fiercely.

"But, Uncle Enos, I was only trying to see —"

"I want it clearly understood here and now," said Uncle Enos, "that I will have no more of this sneaking and spying into my private papers." He thrust the little book into one of the desk drawers, his hand shaking so much that he could hardly turn the key in the lock.

"But, Uncle Enos, I was only —"

167

"Go to your room at once," said Uncle Enos, turning his back on me.

There were twenty-nine rooms at Rest-and-be-thankful, without a soul in any one of them except the study and the kitchen, but Uncle Enos's notions of discipline dated from the days when a naughty child was sent upstairs in disgrace to spend the rest of the afternoon in lonely misery away from his brothers and sisters.

"But, Uncle Enos —"

"Did you hear what I said?"

It was obviously useless even to reply. I got to my feet with what dignity I could and trailed away unhappily up the stairs.

I went slowly, running one finger absent-mindedly along the polished rail of the banister and frowning to myself. I was trying to remember the exact shape of the coat of arms which had been stamped on the brown leather cover of the little book.

The work must have been skillfully done; the gold was slightly rubbed and faded, but even after a hundred years or so, the small impression had looked perfectly clear. I could still see it as I had in that single flash before Uncle Enos snatched it away from me. The shield had been blank except for three little points like rayed stars clustered in the upper left-hand corner. And under the shield itself was the usual narrow twist of ribbon divided into stiff folds to carry the motto. Three folds, with a word on each: Latin words. *Quod* something — I shut my eyes for an instant in my effort to concentrate — *quod . . . quod desidero obtineo.*

"But that isn't possible!" I thought, shaking my head as though to untangle it. "I can't have remembered properly. What would Uncle Enos be doing with one of Peaceable Sherwood's books? Unless, perhaps . . ."

I paused on the landing and glanced speculatively up at the great Copley portrait gleaming down from the wall. After a moment I even murmured coaxingly, "Did he ever really get what he wanted, Barbara?" But this time there was not even a whisper or a rustle in reply. The painted hand remained lifted in the way it always was to tuck back the dark curl that was blowing out of the crimson hood; and the painted eyes continued to look over my head in the way they always did, as if they were smiling about some secret of their own.

The Punch Bowl

"In Scarlet Town, where I was born,
There was a fair maid dwellin' — "

I crooned happily to myself, giving the big chocolate
pot one last swish through the soapy water before I
lifted it out to drain. It skittered dangerously
against the edge of the dishpan and I snatched it
back, glancing around the pantry door to make sure
Uncle Enos had not seen what happened — Uncle
Enos already had quite enough on his mind that
morning without the chocolate pot to add to the rest
of his difficulties. It was the Fourth of July, and the
Fourth of July meant that the Independence Day
Ball was hanging over his head again.

The Independence Day Ball always took place
annually on the Fourth of July for the simple reason
that it had taken place annually on the Fourth of
July ever since the first Richard Grahame had given
that original Independence Day Ball in 1780. Any
other day of the year, I think Uncle Enos would
sooner have cut his own throat than gone to the

trouble of arranging a party. But much as he hated frivolity and disturbance, he hated the thought of breaking a family custom still more — and so, though he had grumbled and rumbled and sputtered like a volcano for days beforehand, in the end he had set his teeth and grimly got on with the job, finding what satisfaction he could out of making it a mercilessly accurate reproduction of an eighteenth-century "assembly," from the first curl in my powdered wig down to the last clove in the cold Virginia ham.

By the morning of the Day itself, Rest-and-be-thankful had reached an almost hysterical pitch of excitement. Uncle Enos had harried the entire household out of their beds at sunrise, fretting about the weather, which was perfect; his costume, which he wished to send back because he thought the design on the lace was modern; and the last-minute preparations for the evening, which he changed so often that by ten o'clock none of us knew whether we were on our heads or our heels. I was in the big pantry off the dining room, washing a set of ancestral china and wondering whether there was any chance of talking Uncle Enos into adding a few modern dances to the relentless program of minuets and Virginia reels he had laid out for the entertainment of his company. Through the open door of the pantry I could see Christopher Seven in the dining room arranging chairs against the wall, and Petunia steadying a ladder while Gladiola set fresh candles in the chandelier. Uncle Enos was out of sight somewhere down by the sideboard, passionately trying to persuade the six hired waiters he had imported for the occasion that it was absolutely necessary for them to put on the apricot coats and black satin knee breeches all the Grahame men-servants had worn as livery back in the eighteenth century.

"S-ss-sst! Peggy!"

I spun around so hastily that the chocolate pot skidded out of my hands again and toppled over the edge of the drainboard altogether. Pat, outside in the garden, swung himself halfway through the low window, caught it before it fell, and returned it to me.

"Good lord, of all people!" I gasped. "How on earth did you get here?"

"Betsy," said Pat complacently, climbing up on the window sill and settling down there comfortably with his shoulder against the jamb. "I was going over to do a little work at the Goshen Historical Society, but it seems all the colonials around here are celebrating some sort of local holiday and the place is closed. Would you care to come for a nice long ride with me instead? There's an old inn over at Chester that I really ought to see."

"Ride!" I echoed bitterly. "Have you gone clean crazy, coming straight up to the house like this? There are only ten people on the other side of that door, if you're interested."

172

"People? I thought it was a herd of maddened elephants," said Pat, cocking his head to listen to the tumult in the dining room. Gladiola was imploring her sister not to joggle the ladder. Petunia was shrilly denying that she had ever joggled anything. Christopher Seven was ordering them to make less noise. The six hired waiters were all explaining together that the rules of their particular union did not allow them to wear "none of dese fency costooms," and Uncle Enos was insisting frenziedly that they put them on at once if they felt the slightest pride or reverence for the glorious past of their native land.

"Oooooh! A party!" said Pat. "Am I invited?"

"You couldn't get in," I retorted, laughing. "You don't know what an exclusive and patriotic gathering this is going to be! Uncle Enos has hired three large footmen on purpose to make sure that all you redcoats are kept outside."

I might have known that that was the wrong line to take with him. Pat merely clasped his hands around one knee and began to smile thoughtfully.

"Three large footmen, I think you said?" he inquired casually.

"Now, Pat! Please! If you have any ridiculous notion —"

"I never have ridiculous notions," said Pat, in a deeply injured voice. "I was only going to remark that I'll dance with you before the night has ended,

173

my proud beauty," he added, and vanished like a shadow over the window sill just as Uncle Enos appeared at the pantry door.

Uncle Enos was looking rather harrowed and tragic and muttering under his breath. Christopher Seven, also looking harrowed and tragic, was coming up behind him carrying the great silver punch bowl designed by Paul Revere that Uncle Enos really valued more than anything else in the house. It was usually kept locked up somewhere in his study. Even I myself had seen it only once before, on the truly frightful occasion when the minister's wife attempted to borrow it for the Lemonade Table at the church fair.

"Set it down there," said Uncle Enos, pointing to a small table in the corner of the dining room as magnificently as the Revolutionary colonel showing the American gunners how to blow down his own house at the Battle of Yorktown, "and if it's dented, then I suppose it will just have to be dented, that's all. Now pull that screen around here in front of the table — so. Peggy!"

"Yes, Uncle Enos? Did you want me?"

Uncle Enos sighed heavily. "Yes, I'm afraid I do," he said. "While going over the family records of the Independence Day Balls last night, I discovered that in the eighteenth century the guests were always served punch from this particular bowl by the daughter of the house herself. Under ordinary circumstances, as you know, nothing could compel me to risk the bowl in any such manner; but since custom requires it, and since you are in all respects the daughter of the house —"

"I will be delighted to serve the punch for you, Uncle Enos, of course," I finished promptly, knowing what was expected of me. "Where do you want me to stand? The bowl would look pretty under the lights at the end of the dining-room table." I had a sudden fascinating vision of myself posed between two silver candelabra in my flowered satin gown, manipulating the ladle gracefully before a crowd of admiring eyes.

Uncle Enos shook his head.

"Not in the eighteenth century," he said. "In the eighteenth century it was customary to serve the punch at this small table here behind the screen."

"But, Uncle Enos!" I protested. "That's the most inconvenient and out-of-the-way corner in the whole room. Nobody will even be able to see me back there."

"Fortunate child!" agreed Uncle Enos, with another heavy sigh. "Lord! what wouldn't I give for your chance to spend the entire evening in an out-of-the-way corner where nobody would even be able to see me!"

"The — did you say the *entire* evening, Uncle Enos? You don't mean during the dancing and everything?"

"Of course I mean the dancing and everything."

"But if you don't mind very much, I'd really rather —"

"Just think what a nice quiet time you'll have," said Uncle Enos encouragingly.

I was thinking about what a nice quiet time I was going to have, but even then I did not realize exactly how long or quiet the night would actually be. Very few guests found their way into my hidden corner, and those who did evidently spread the word that the punch Uncle Enos had concocted with his own hands according to a recipe he had found in a colonial cookbook was not so successful as he thought it was, for presently hour after hour began to go by without a single soul appearing but a solitary Greek waiter, who stayed only long enough to take away the dirty glasses and bring me a chicken salad from the supper table. Uncle Enos had not had his own way about one thing at least — the waiter was wearing a standard dinner jacket and long black modern trousers — but unfortunately I was not a waiter and had no powerful union to protect me against other people's whims. I could hear music and laughter from the far end of the room, and (by leaning forward and craning my neck) could occasionally catch a glimpse of a flashing knee buckle or a brocaded hoop skirt swirling past on the terrace or going down the steps to the moonlit garden. Otherwise, as far as the Independence Day Ball was concerned, I might

176

just as well have been in bed and asleep.

I had my elbows on the table and was about to shed a few miserable, shamefaced tears into the chicken salad when the sound of a light step made me glance up to find a slim young man standing in the shadow of the heavy screen and languidly gazing down at the punch bowl. The inadequate light of the eighteenth-century candles did not reach his face. I could see only that he was tall and slender and rather sloppily dressed — his black satin knee breeches fitted him badly, and the cuffs of his apricot coat came almost to the knuckles of his thin, long-fingered hands. For one moment it flashed across my mind that it might be Pat, somehow rigged out in one of the fancy costumes which the six waiters had disdainfully left lying in the kitchen. Then the intruder turned, caught my eye on him, and bowed apologetically.

"I beg your pardon," he said, in a slow, rather lazy voice I had never heard before. "I fear I was standing here admiring your punch bowl. I had very little chance to examine it properly the last time I saw it."

He must, I thought, be one of the young scholars Uncle Enos occasionally permitted to work with his collections. "Oh," I said politely, "you've seen the punch bowl before, then?"

"I saw it," explained the stranger, gravely, "on the night I served the punch."

"I — I'm afraid you must be mistaken," I corrected him. "At least, Uncle Enos tells me that only the daughter of the house —"

"This occurred some time before your Uncle Enos was born. Well over a hundred and fifty years ago, to be exact."

I was by now so accustomed to these sudden returns from the past that I did not even start. "You're not by any chance the fool ancestor who began the fool custom of leaving the punch bowl in this particular corner?" I demanded.

"No. Only the fool ancestor who didn't get himself hanged on a fool gallows because the punch bowl happened to be in that particular corner," retorted the young man, placidly. "At your service, Miss Grahame." He took a step forward out of the shadow to bow to me again, and the light from the candles fell suddenly across his face: a thin, curiously attractive face with lazily drooping eyes and an unmistakable dreamy smile.

"But I don't understand," I stammered. "What were you doing here? And how in the world did you ever get out of the Goshen jail in the first place?"

It took rather longer than I thought it would (said Peaceable Sherwood modestly), considering that the Goshen jail in those days was by no means the most perfect stronghold ever devised by the hand of man. Indeed, there was not a lock in the place I could not have opened blindfold with the handle of a prison spoon any dark night of the week. One of my followers — old Timothy — had begun life as a thief in London and was always yearning for the good old days; he used to come away from raids with his pockets full of locks and bolts and teach me tricks with them to keep his hand in while we were hiding up in the hills.

Unfortunately, however, Dick must have warned the authorities to expect something of the sort. I had hardly recovered from the effects of Aunt Susanna's sleeping drops before a village blacksmith had entered my cell and was fastening my right wrist securely to the wall with an iron chain just short enough to keep me from reaching the barred window at one end of the room or the grated door at the other.

If I had been an ordinary prisoner of war it would probably never have happened — officers on both sides were frequently allowed an amazing amount of freedom if they gave their word of honor (parole, it was called) that they would make no effort to escape. But then I was not exactly an ordinary prisoner of war. I was a notorious marauder who had kept the whole countryside in a state of terror for almost a year, and while my uniform was enough to prevent the county officials from actually hanging me, there was no reason on earth why they should go out of their way to make my confinement easy or pleasant.

"There!" said the blacksmith proudly, rising from his knees and mopping his forehead when the work was over, "I reckon that'll keep you put for a while, son."

"I reckon it will," I agreed with him ruefully.

It did. Old Timothy had neglected to teach me how to open a shackle, even supposing that I could have managed it with only my left hand, and the chain was too strong to break by simple force. I thought of trying to wear it through by rubbing one link against another — I even calculated just how long the process would take: sixty-eight years, three months, and eleven days. But as this seemed rather a long time to wait, I decided in the end that I had better do nothing at all but behave admirably until the authorities grew ashamed of their foolish caution and took the chain for some more violent and rebellious prisoner.

Happily, as you see, I am an unusually slender and harmless-looking individual, even at the best of times. It was not very difficult for me to give the impression that I was reduced to a state of complete lassitude and despair. I drooped and pined; I almost never spoke; and when I was not dragging myself wearily from the door to the window like a caged animal, I was lying stretched out on my heap of

straw, gazing pathetically at a distant strip of sky.

It would probably have been even more effective to remain on the straw altogether — but there was no sense in weakening myself so much that I would be unfit for the road when I got to it at last. I worked out the exact distance from the door to the window, and my jailers might have been surprised to learn how many measured miles I actually walked back and forth between the two every day. But I took great care that the jailers never saw anything but a broken spirit creeping in restless misery around the floor; and it was not long before visitors were beginning to ask them almost incredulously if that could really be the notorious Peaceable Sherwood at all?

There were a good many visitors to stare at the notorious Peaceable Sherwood — it was years before I could enjoy a wild-beast show afterwards — and they were all very much alike. Little wiry men usually asked the jailer why I hadn't been hanged on the spot. Large substantial ones generally remarked that I didn't look like much of a handful to them. Grey-haired elderly ladies always cried, "Oh, the poor boy!" while the young and fluttery type preferred to inquire sentimentally if I truly had to be kept tied up like that. Everybody without exception agreed that I was not at all what they had expected, and ended by wondering why such a pother had ever been made about me.

Still, I must say for the authorities that they were

182

very slow to relax their vigilance. It was not until the night of July the third that the prisoner I had been longing for finally arrived — an enormous, hulking bull of a man, blind drunk and fighting mad. He broke loose at one end of the corridor and dragged three guards and the chief jailer all the way down it before he was brought to earth at last just outside my cell. The chief jailer disentangled himself from the struggling heap and came across to the door.

I was stretched out as usual on my pile of straw, apparently too listless even to turn my head and look at the riot still going on only ten feet away from me. The chief jailer watched me speculatively for a moment, nursing a mangled shoulder with one hand and wiping at a black eye with the other. Then he swung around and regarded the new arrival, who was thrashing on the floor like a stranded whale, with one guard holding down his legs and the rest clinging desperately to his shoulders.

"Put him in here and chain him up," he ordered curtly. "Yes, that chain, you fool — do you see any other chain in that cell? Peaceable Sherwood? I'm tired of hearing about Peaceable Sherwood! Turn him loose in the cell for the night. — Which one of you said 'Where'll he be by morning?' Where does he look as if he's going to be by morning, I ask you — a hundred and fifty miles away?"

I was, to be exact, only seven and a half miles

away by morning, furiously covering as much highway as I could before daylight made it unsafe for a somewhat bedraggled officer in a British uniform to be seen on the open road. I was headed east and downriver for my old hunting grounds in the hills and forests. Once I got there, it would be a simple matter to slip through the American lines and reach the British army beyond them at New York. When the sun rose, I struck off into the shelter of the woods, found a brook, stripped off my boots, and "broke my scent" by wading upstream almost a mile against the force of the current. I knew every nook and cranny of the country so well that I was fairly certain of eluding any human pursuers, but there was always the chance that they might set hounds on me if they discovered my escape while the trail was still fresh enough to follow.

It was maddeningly slow going: the brook, though reasonably free from rocks and hidden pitfalls, wound and twisted and doubled on its course so often that I could have made three miles on dry land to every one that I made in the water. It was also, I realized with dismay, gradually leading me out of the woods into open fields and cultivated farm land. I could hear a sheep dog barking irritably somewhere far off beyond the trees at my right — and then a distant woman calling faintly: "Boys! Boys! Hurry yourselves! You ought to be dressed this minute!"

"Coming!" answered two other voices together, so loud and so unexpectedly close that I jumped and almost dropped one of the riding boots I was carrying under my arm into the water. The "boys" were evidently swimming or playing by the brook just around the next bend. Another twenty yards and I would have blundered straight into them.

I waited until the last spatter of feet breaking through the underbrush had died away, and then crept cautiously forward to find that around the next bend the brook had been dammed to make a quiet pool, pleasantly screened by sumac. Abandoned on the bank lay a chunk of yellow soap, a rough hucka-back towel, and a clumsy razor. The "boys" had apparently been interrupted while they were experimenting with their father's shaving tackle, and had gone away so hastily that they had forgotten to take it with them. The only question was, how soon would they come back for it?

The sensible thing to do was obviously to praise heaven for a narrow escape and leave as fast as my feet would carry me. On the other hand, I had not had a proper bath for six months. I was shaking with weariness, crawling with mosquitoes, plastered from head to foot with dirt and prison muck. I had never felt so hot or filthy in my life. The boys would surely take some time to dress, and perhaps if I were only quick . . .

Unfortunately, I was not quite quick enough. I

had finished shaving and was splashing luxuriously in the center of the pool when a startled cry from the opposite bank made me glance up to see a wiry lad of about sixteen petrified on the water's edge and gaping across at me in open-mouthed astonishment. A second boy was making his way down the rocks to join him. He was taller than his companion and perhaps two years older, with a lowering, brutal face and the heavy, dangerous shoulders of a wrestler. There was an ugly cut on the angle of his jaw — the kind caused by a razor in inexperienced hands.

"What you doing in there?" he demanded unpleasantly.

"Washing," I replied politely, wondering if the scarlet sleeve sticking out from the clump of bushes on the other side of the pool looked as much like a sumac flower as I hoped it did.

"And who told you you could wash in that there pond? You come straight out before I drag you and march yourself up to the house. My Paw'll tend to you, he —"

"George!" the younger boy cut in excitedly. "George! He's got our hunk of soap — and he's been shaving with Paw's razor too!"

"I didn't know it was your Paw's razor," I retorted. "And besides, if a man leaves his razor in plain sight on the bank of a pool where anyone can find it, he ought to be grateful when the first poor tramping soldier who comes by simply uses it instead of stealing it — as he will doubtless agree when I explain the matter to him."

I saw by the glances that the two exchanged that they were not in the least anxious that Paw should learn that his razor had been on the bank of the pool or anywhere else within miles of the place.

"Reckon we had really ought to take him up to the house, George?" wavered the younger one uncertainly. "If he's a soldier like he says and hasn't done no harm —"

But George was made of sterner stuff. "I don't like his looks," he insisted stubbornly. "How do we know he ain't no thief or maybe even one of them outlaws broke loose out of the Goshen jail? He looks mighty white-faced to be any soldier to me, and anyway, if he is one, why ain't he with the army where he belongs?"

"I'm on my way back to the army now," I replied — it did not seem necessary to point out which particular army it was. "And I wager you wouldn't have any more sunburn than I do if you'd been struck down at Christmas and confined to your bedroom ever since. I've only been able to move about since yesterday." How marvelous a thing is the exact truth, properly manipulated!

"What's your name?" was the next question.

"William Shakespeare," I retorted recklessly.

"Never knew anybody named that," said George

with suspicion. "Leastwise, they ain't no Orange County family I ever heard tell of."

"They're well known in my part of the world," I responded amiably, splashing a little in the water.

"Anyhow, I got a good mind —"

"Oh, come on, George!" the younger boy interrupted him. "Are you going to stand there on the bank gabbing at him *all* day? He's told you who he is, and Paw's razor's safe, and you know well as I do you ain't going to lug him out of no pond with your best clothes on, and we'll miss our chance at Restenbeethankful if we don't get moving. I bet Joe Titterton's boys is there already."

"On your way to Rest-and-be-thankful?" I inquired carelessly.

"It's the big party they're giving tonight because it's the Fourth of July and the Colonel's getting married," explained the younger boy. "We didn't think they was going to open up the house again till after the war, but Joe Titterton told us that old man Grahame got back special for the wedding, and there was guests coming from all over the county, maybe even the General from West Point and everybody, and they was short of help on account of the house being shut up so long and the men away with the army, so maybe we might get in to wash dishes or something, and George reckons he might even get to wait on people if he washed up good and took Paw's razor to shave off his —"

188

"Oh, shut your big mouth, Johnny!" George broke in, redfaced and exasperated. "Do you have to tell *everything* you know? You said we got to hurry, didn't you? And as for you — " he swung around on me, "I ain't got no time to fool with you now, but I give you fair warning to get out of that water and take yourself off of this here property quicker than scat if you know what's good for you," and with one last glare, he swept the towel and razor into his pocket, took his brother by the shoulder, and tramped away.

I came up the bank and lay down there to dry myself in the sunshine while I thought over the situation. Rest-and-be-thankful was not very far off, and it lay directly on my line of march. That meant I ought to alter my course. If the Grahames were entertaining "the General from West Point" and no doubt half of the other American officers stationed in the County, it would be suicidal to go within miles of the place.

Or would it? One of the lessons I had learned during my career as an outlaw was that the safest hiding place is usually under the sheriff's bed. There was bound to be a good deal of turmoil and scurry and confusion at a "big party." I might be able to slip past under the cover of darkness. I might even be able to steal some food — and I was already getting very hungry — or find a horse unguarded in the stables. And now I came to think of it, Dick would probably not be marrying his **Eleanor** at all if it were not for me. In a manner of speaking, I had made the match myself; and while I was hardly in a position to offer them my formal congratulations, it seemed churlish just to go by the house without so much as paying a little call.

And — the real and the only argument — Barbara Grahame was sure to be there. I wanted to see Barbara Grahame again very badly. After all, I had actually known her for only six hours. I had been separated from her now for a good six months, and the war might conceivably go on for another six years. There was not the faintest doubt in my mind that I was going to spend the rest of my life with her as soon as the ink was dry on the peace treaty, but even I could allow that it might really be better to see her and come to a complete understanding on the subject before I had to be off again till the Lord knew when. It was true that at the moment I did not exactly know how I would ever contrive to see her — but all that could take care of itself after I got to Rest-and-be-thankful. *"Quod desidero obtineo,"* I murmured to myself as I put on my coat and melted away into the woods again.

The remainder of the day went by uneventfully. I spent most of it keeping quietly to the hills and the underbrush. Indeed, I passed only one house, late that afternoon — a forest tavern near Rest-and-be-thankful — where I had a glimpse of a slatternly woman hanging out wash on a line, and a crowd of curious country folk gathered around a parcel of mounted soldiers who were refreshing themselves with tankards of beer by the door. Their lieutenant — a large, square-shouldered Southerner I had never seen before — was reading a sort of proclamation aloud from a sheet of paper. I lay up among the trees behind the place and listened. His voice was only too painfully clear.

"Aged about twenty-three," he was saying. "Tall . . . thin . . . blue eyes . . . stronger than he looks . . . signet ring on fourth finger of left hand . . . last seen wearing a dirty regulation tie-wig and uniform of British captain with — "

I looked hungrily at the homespun shirts and sturdy worsted stockings flapping dankly on the slatternly woman's line, and then shook my head sadly. That dirty regulation tie-wig and British uniform were all that stood between me and a sudden unpleasant death on the nearest gallows. An enemy officer found on hostile territory in disguise was by that very fact assumed to be a spy and received the usual punishment provided for such, as my poor friend John André was to discover a few months later when he went upriver on the King's business with Benedict Arnold.

The lieutenant finished reading the description of me, asked the country folk some questions, and rode off with his companions in a cloud of dust. I retreated to a safer hiding place farther back in the woods to wait for nightfall before I started down to Rest-and-be-thankful.

It had been a very warm day, and a little after sunset the heat finally piled up and broke in a brief, violent storm which drifted away toward the river after a minute or two but left everything behind it wet and dripping and chill. I drew a long breath of relief — at least I could be fairly sure that the garden was no longer full of strolling guests out to enjoy the balmy air and the moonlight. It would really have been ridiculous not to take advantage of so much good fortune. The last rumble of thunder had hardly died away before I rose, cut downhill through the woods, crossed a dark field, climbed a wall, and slipped between the trees of the orchard like a shadow.

The garden beyond the orchard was, as I had hoped, deserted. So was the terrace that ran along the front of the house, though it must have been crowded earlier in the evening — I could see cushions littering the steps and scattered wineglasses gleaming on the balustrade in the candlelight pouring from all the long windows. A single liveried servant was straightening the chairs and gathering up the empty glasses on a tray. He moved very slowly, pausing every two seconds to listen to the music or to peer in at the dancers. It seemed centuries before he worked his way down to the far end of the terrace and disappeared from view around the corner of the library, leaving me free to dart up the steps and reach the dense shadow of the great oak which had been left to shade the south windows when the house was built.

I had been in the dark so long that when I first looked in all I could see for an instant was a crazy swirl of lights and colors — candle flames, crystals, gleaming satins, brocades and velvets: crimson, blue, purple, rose, green and gold, all swaying and dipping together in the intricate patterns of the minuet. Then, as my eyes grew more accustomed to the glitter, I began to pick out here and there faces that I recognized. The stout, jolly, red-faced gentleman was old Mr. Shipley, Eleanor's father. The dark, slightly lame man in the general's uniform must be Benedict Arnold from West Point. The boy dancing shyly with the pretty girl was the same Lieutenant Featherstone that I had last seen beating off two of my men with a broken sword during the skirmish at the Beemer Mill. I even had a glimpse of Dick and Eleanor as the music stopped and the groups of dancers began to break up. They were coming down past the window in a knot of acquaintances, all laughing and talking at once. I caught a phrase about "your wedding tomorrow," and then a joke about this being their last real Independence Day that made me shudder and resolve to insist on a strictly private ceremony for myself and Barbara, without any old friends and well-wishers to —

I suddenly threw back my head and listened. I had heard a sound from the distance behind me.

Very faint, very distinct, rising and falling rhythmically on the wet night air: the regular, unmistakable beat of a squadron sweeping down the road at a full gallop. Then, as I turned, the horses' hoofs hesitated, paused, and broke down confusedly. The riders were dismounting at the upper orchard gate.

Not cavalry officers arriving late for the ball — they would have come straight on down the drive and left their horses at the door. There was only one reason why they should have dismounted at the upper gate: they must be intending to make their way quietly up through the orchard and garden, hunting for somebody. And the only person they were likely to be hunting for was an escaped prisoner of war, badly wanted by the authorities at the Goshen jail, aged about twenty-three, tall, thin, blue-eyed, stronger than he looked, a signet ring on the fourth finger of his left hand, last seen wearing a dirty regulation tie-wig and the uniform of a captain in the British army with —

The lighted terrace was obviously no place for me. I shot out of the shade of the oak even faster than I had shot into it, put one hand on the balustrade for a quick spring into the shrubbery — and caught sight of the liveried servant with the tray of glasses, coming back around the corner of the library wing, walking briskly and humming a tune under his breath. I had most stupidly forgotten that he would have to return that way to take his dirty glasses to the scullery.

Run — and he would have every soul in the place down on me before I could escape across the lawn. Stay where I was and put a bold face on the matter — and there was a chance, one very thin chance, that he might take me for some prisoner of war who had been permitted to come to the festivities on parole. I relaxed suddenly against the balustrade, like an unconcerned guest who had stepped out for a mouthful of fresh air, yawned carelessly as he approached . . . and then saw to my complete dismay that he was nobody on earth but my old acquaintance George, magnificently tricked out in a powdered wig, an apricot-colored coat, and black satin knee breeches that were rather too large for him. We recognized one another at the same moment.

If George had only had enough sense to leap back and shout for help, he could have sent me back to my pile of straw in the Goshen jail without further difficulty. Instead, the unspeakable fool simply made a blind rush, dropped his tray of glasses, and lashed out recklessly with his fists. He evidently remembered how meekly I had behaved when he found me in the pool and thought that he was not going to have any trouble with me. It was a perfectly natural mistake. Most people made it the first time they met me.

"I'm sorry, George," I murmured apologetically, and hit him.

George flung up both hands and went down in a heap. His head struck the sharp edge of the balustrade with a sickening crack; he rolled over, and lay still among the scattered fragments of the wine-glasses.

The whisper of violins and the tap of dancing feet went on without interruption in the ballroom. The guests were making so much noise of their own that a little more on the terrace had passed unnoticed. The soldiers who had dismounted at the gate were not yet in sight. That meant they were still searching for me in the grounds on their way up to the house — and the orchards and the shrubberies must be full of them. I could hardly hope to escape now. George had delayed me just long enough to make it almost impossible.

He still lay where he had fallen, an ugly sight, quite unconscious. His own mother would not have recognized his face, cut and hacked and bleeding from his plunge into the broken wineglasses. I frowned suddenly and began to turn over one of the broken glasses meditatively with the toe of my boot.

It might be possible. It could by no stretch of the imagination be called a brilliant plan, and if I were caught it would certainly mean the end of me, but it might be possible . . . I took off my coat.

Fortunately, George was still young and no larger below the shoulders than I was. My boots and breeches fitted him easily enough. The coat, of course, was a narrow squeeze, but I left it unbuttoned and hoped for the best. I had just settled his powdered wig on my own head, and was twisting off my signet ring to slip over the fourth finger of his left hand when there was a sudden rattle of spurs on the flagstones, and a gruff Southern voice called from the garden behind me: "You there, have you seen a — Hey! what's that you've got?"

The large lieutenant I had seen reading the proclamation at the tavern was standing at the foot of the steps, a cluster of troopers crowding at his back, all of them staring at the British officer and the liveried servant on the terrace. They were, happily, unable to perceive that it was no longer quite the same British officer and liveried servant who had been there five minutes before.

I dropped the signet ring into my pocket and rose twittering to my feet, the perfect image of a distracted young footman only too thankful to surrender a difficult problem into the hands of the proper authorities.

"I don't quite know myself, sir," I bleated uncertainly. "I was just going back to the scullery with my tray of glasses, sir, and I saw this person hiding there under the oak on the terrace, and he seemed to be a British officer, sir, so I knocked him down, sir, and I do hope I haven't done no harm, sir, if — " The rest of the sentence was lost as the large lieutenant swept me aside with one wave of his arm and went down on his knee beside George's prostrate body.

"I do hope I haven't done no harm, sir," I repeated pitifully.

"Harm!" said the large lieutenant, with a snort. "You've probably put in the best night's work you ever did in your life, son. You know who this is? Well, it's Peaceable Sherwood."

"Oh, sir!"

"Yes, that's it — if he's the one I think he is. Let's see. Tall: correct. Thin — well, he isn't fat anyway: correct. Blue eyes: correct. Signet ring: missing. Look, son, what was that thing I saw you putting in your pocket when we came up the steps? Well, well, never mind, keep it, I suppose you deserve it, let's just not say anything more about it. Dirty regulation tie-wig and British uniform: correct. Looks like we've found him all right, boys. Still, to make sure — any of you-all ever seen him so close that you'd recognize him again? Step forward!"

Rather to my relief, nobody stepped forward.

"Colonel Grahame or Miss Barbara could tell right away, sir," suggested a voice helpfully. " 'Twouldn't take me a minute to run around to the back of the house and fetch one of them, sir."

The lieutenant glanced in at the glittering crowd

and shook his head. "I reckon that won't be necessary," he said doubtfully. "Colonel Grahame wouldn't thank us for breaking up his party and making a riot the night before his wedding — not with the General here and everybody — and after all, it isn't as if there were *two* British officers loose in Orange County with captains' uniforms and dirty wigs and blue eyes and all the rest of it. Suppose we just pick him up quiet and easy, and get out of here before anybody — "

"Why, Lieutenant Carter! I thought you said you were on duty tonight and couldn't come?"

Lieutenant Carter turned on his heel and bowed profoundly as a slender figure in yellow closed the long window behind her and came out to us, the candlelight shimmering over her fan and her dress and the brilliants starring her hair. At the sound of her voice, I drew one deep breath and retreated modestly to the shade of the oak tree.

"Nothing at all worth troubling you with, Miss Barbara ma'am," Lieutenant Carter was explaining apologetically. "Only one of the Britishers up at the Goshen jail who escaped last night and was trying to get down to New York. I'm afraid we had to break into your garden to catch him."

"Into our garden?" echoed Barbara. "But of all the foolish places for him to . . . Oh! Who — who is he?"

"Well, it's odd, Miss Barbara, but he seems to be

199

that same marauder you and the Colonel captured last Christmas — you remember him? Sherwood? Captain Peaceable Sherwood?"

The fan Barbara was carrying suddenly shimmered a little in the candlelight, as if the fingers that held it had tightened their grip, but her answer came in precisely the right tone of polite surprise and interest.

"Indeed? How very astonishing!" she said. "I hope the poor man isn't badly hurt?"

"Oh, he'll wake up again all right and tight back in the Goshen jail," replied Lieutenant Carter cheerfully. "Seems he had a fight with one of your own servants, who found him hiding on the terrace and knocked him down — that man over there yonder, under the tree."

Barbara turned and glanced at me. The friendly shadow of the oak lay thick across my face, but unfortunately not quite thick enough to conceal the shape of my head and the outline of my shoulders. I saw Barbara's lips part and her eyes widen suddenly in bewilderment.

"Are you sure you've caught the right man, Lieutenant Carter?" she inquired, with a new and rather strange note in her voice.

"Fairly sure, Miss Barbara," said Lieutenant Carter complacently. "Of course, though, we had only the printed description to go by, and — well, I wonder if it would be asking too much of you,

Miss Barbara, now you're out here anyway, just to glance at him, and see if you can't positively identify him for us? Blood doesn't make you faint, does it?"

I knew what the answer was going to be even before Barbara made it.

"Not in the least, sir. If you wouldn't mind stepping to one side a little — ?" She bent forward, guarding her skirts delicately from the shards of broken glass, and surveyed the miserable George for a long moment in silence. It was the sort of silence I could imagine falling over the crowd on the Goshen green as the rope tightened slowly around my neck.

Then Barbara straightened up again and turned back to Lieutenant Carter.

"I can't *swear* to him, of course," she said, slowly and deliberately. "His own sweetheart couldn't swear to that face just now, I'm afraid. But I will say that I'm sure I've seen him before. He looks very familiar — " her eyes went around the circle of intent faces and came to rest again, as if by chance, on mine: "very familiar indeed. And he *is* wearing Captain Sherwood's coat. I remember that patch on the left elbow distinctly."

"That last fact alone would be quite enough to satisfy us, I assure you," said the lieutenant heartily. "Pick him up, boys. The sooner he goes back where he belongs, the better. I really don't know how to thank you properly, Miss Barbara. If there's any way my men or I can show our appreciation — "

"Very easily. Do you think you could possibly get him off the grounds before anyone else sees him? After all, fights and escaping prisoners and blood at a dance where the guests are supposed to be enjoying themselves the night before a wedding — " She broke off with an appealing little gesture of her hands.

"Not a soul will even know we've been here," promised Lieutenant Carter handsomely.

"How very kind of you, sir — and I only wish you could stay on for the dancing." She gave him one of her delightful smiles and turned back to the long window. "Come, George," she added, over one shoulder.

"George — Oh Lord, yes, I'd forgotten about him." The lieutenant stopped short halfway down the steps, fumbled in his coat, and tossed me a silver coin, which I caught neatly and put in my pocket with a grateful bow.

"And I only wish it was more, son," he added cordially. "But I'll tell them up at Goshen that you're the one who ought to get the reward, if there should happen to be any. Meanwhile" — he bowed again to Barbara as he turned to rejoin his followers — "I'm sure Miss Barbara here will take good care of you and see you're treated the way you deserve to be."

"You may be certain of that, Lieutenant Carter," said Barbara sweetly, giving him another dazzling smile as she closed her fan with a snap and swept me in through the window. I followed her in silence past the fringes of the dance and down the room to a secluded corner where a silver punch bowl stood on a small table, flanked and cut off from the rest of the dining parlor by a heavy screen. Here she halted and turned fiercely to confront me.

"Now, I'll attend to *you*," she said dangerously. "Have you lost your mind, coming straight back to the house like this? Didn't you remember that I was the one who put you in that jail in the first place?"

"Oh, yes," I assured her. "All the Sherwoods have memories like elephants. We never forget."

"And what possessed you to take off that uniform?" wailed Barbara. "Are you completely mad? Don't you know they'll hang you now if they catch you?"

"Something of the sort did pass through my head," I admitted. "I even composed about half of a farewell speech (to be recited on the gallows) in the time you spent looking at George to see if you couldn't positively identify him."

"Oh, will you stop talking nonsense!" She wrung her hands distressfully together. "Be quiet and let me think! Dear Lord, what am I going to do with you? What in the world am I going to do with you?"

"That," I answered, finding a place where I could lean comfortably against the corner of the table, "is the exact question which I came to Rest-and-be-thankful especially to ask you. What *are* you going to do with me? You may perhaps remember that at Christmas time I did myself the honor of asking for your hand in — "

A voice from the other side of the screen interrupted me. It was a gay, careless voice, very distinct above the low laughter and the music.

"Oh, Felton! Just one moment, please! Have you chanced to see my sister anywhere about? There's something I have to tell her."

The reply came without an instant's hesitation. "I thought I had a glimpse of her just now going back to the corner with the punch bowl, sir."

All the color faded suddenly out of Barbara's cheeks and lips, leaving her face so white that the gray eyes looked black.

"It's Dick," she whispered. "Oh heaven help us, it's Dick, and he's coming over here."

"Why not?" I inquired cordially. "It's his own party, isn't it? I'm only a simple country boy named George who's come in from Paw's farm to work here for the night. He won't even look at me — nobody ever looks at the footmen. All I have to do is turn my back and start ladling punch into the cups. You see? Now, where was I? Oh, yes . . . the honor of asking for your hand in marriage. Unfortunately, however, I failed to catch your reply, owing to circumstances beyond my control, so — "

"Will you be quiet!" hissed Barbara frantically.

I dipped up a ladleful of punch, and out of the tail of my eye, saw Dick appear around the edge of the screen, his arm linked through Eleanor Shipley's and his dress epaulettes gleaming under the light of the candles. I had been quite right: his glance swept past me as if I had been a piece of the furniture and went directly to his sister.

"Heard the news?" he inquired hilariously. "Major Ambrose was telling me. He said he heard them crying it in a tavern on his way down. Peaceable Sherwood's broken out of the Goshen jail at last — and I thought I'd best warn you, so you won't be taken unawares when he comes after you."

"And truly kind of you, Dick, only a trifle behindhand," retorted Barbara provokingly, "seeing that he's come already — and gone back again, as a matter of fact."

"Come already! and . . . what did you say?"

"Gone back again. Lieutenant Carter found him and arrested him while he was hiding in the garden. About seven minutes ago, I think, if you wish me to be exact."

Dick uttered a howl of skepticism and derision. "Tell me a story I can swallow!" he hooted. "And don't fancy you're going to make me believe that any lieutenant just picked Peaceable up and took him away without rousing the house or creating the least disturbance that reached your brother's ears."

"Precisely what he did do. I asked him not to interrupt the dancing and excite the guests."

"Wait a minute! What are you talking about now? You asked him?"

"I asked him."

"*You* were there?"

"I was there. Perhaps you're not aware that it's possible to see that end of the terrace from this small table by the screen? Perceiving a number of strangers by one of the windows, I naturally stepped outside myself, and there I found a man in a British uniform unconscious and bleeding from a bad blow on the head. Lieutenant Carter and his troops were in the act of examining the body. He asked me to identify it for them. I did so to the best of my ability."

"Well, well, well!" Dick gave a long, ungentlemanly whistle, then broke down helplessly into laughter. "Asked *you* to identify him, did they?" he gasped. "My poor, poor Barbara! You do have the worst luck with that man of yours, don't you?"

"He isn't any man of mine," said Barbara indignantly.

"No? Why was he hiding in our garden, then? It's not a place hunted fugitives usually head for. You'd think a man with Peaceable's brains and experience could have found a hundred better holes."

"That's not for me to say."

"Now, don't be spiteful, Barbara. Tell your

brother, like a good little girl. What did he come to bring you? The wedding ring?"

"Once and for all, Richard Grahame, there is no question of my marrying him."

"Is there not? Who spent the last six months sitting at her window and looking wistfully down the Goshen road?"

"Dick, be quiet!" cried Barbara sharply.

"Who made me throw away half my winter trying to get him released or exchanged? — and what a fine waste of time that was! I told you to begin with that they'd sooner turn the devil loose."

"It was only because I was grateful to him for saving my life."

"Well, I was grateful too, but it didn't make me stop my horse and gaze at a jail as if it were my hope of heaven whenever I went up to town."

"I never did any such — "

"Who always gets what he wants, Barbara?"

"Dick, you are becoming impossible!" broke in Eleanor Shipley, laughing. "Can't you see there's a footman over there who can hear every word you say? Stop teasing your sister this instant and go back to your dance! They'll be making up another set in a moment. I can hear the musicians now."

"Eleanor, you are beginning to sound wifely already."

"This instant," said Eleanor firmly.

"And I'll walk with you as far as the supper

table," said Barbara. "It's high time I sent the footmen away to the kitchen for their own supper, poor
things. You, George," she added, as she moved away,
"come along to the butler's pantry as soon as you've
finished filling those cups."

I carefully finished filling the cups — to give Barbara time enough to clear any real footmen out of
the way — and then followed. It was only a few feet
along the wall from the screen to the door of the
pantry, and the new dance was just reaching its
height. Nobody even glanced up at me as I slipped
by and closed the door quietly behind me. The
pantry was empty, and Barbara was coming from the
back hall to the kitchen with a loaf of bread in one
hand and a plate of cold tongue and chicken in the
other.

"The cook says there won't be any baked beans
till Saturday," she apologized, giving me the plate.
"Eat this now, while I cut you a little bread and
cheese to take with you when you go. I thought you
must be hungry. How long has it been since you've
had anything at all?"

"Quite a while," I murmured vaguely, devouring
cold chicken with more appreciation than politeness.
"How did you ever happen to remember that I
might be hungry? But of course, you would. Will
you mind very much if I run myself into serious
difficulties now and again after we are married, just
for the pleasure of seeing you rise to an occasion?"

Barbara did not answer. She was very busy rummaging through the table drawer for a knife to cut the bread and cheese.

"Christopher's down at the stable now saddling a horse for you," she told me. "I said you were feeling weary and knocked up after your fight with Peaceable Sherwood, and had asked for the loan of a mount to take you home."

I did not answer, and there was a moment of silence while Barbara cut bread and cheese and I finished demolishing the plateful of cold tongue and chicken. Then I rose, stretching, and wandered over to the low window to have a look at the night. The moon was beginning to shine vaguely somewhere behind the clouds, but the wet garden was still deserted, and my road seemed clear.

"What are you going to do with me, Barbara?"

There was another moment of silence.

"Well, with a good horse, you ought to be out of reach before Lieutenant Carter even arrives at the Goshen jail," said Barbara at last, rather briskly and firmly, her eyes on the bread and cheese. "Of course, he's sure to make trouble and raise questions when he finds it's only George, but — "

"I didn't ask you what you were going to do with me, my love. I only wanted to know: what are you going to do with *me?*"

"But he will admit," Barbara went on, as if she had not even heard me speak, "that the man I examined was so cut and mauled that I couldn't swear to his face. No one is likely to blame a young and inexperienced girl for such a natural mistake."

"Why did you spend the last six months sitting at your window and looking wistfully down the Goshen road?"

"It will be more difficult," continued Barbara, still without heeding me in the least, "to explain why I failed to recognize you later when I brought you into the house; but I can say — "

"Why did you make your poor brother waste half his winter in those perfectly ridiculous efforts to get me released or exchanged?"

"I can say," repeated Barbara, "that we were no sooner inside the door than you complained of feeling unwell after your struggle and begged me for permission to leave. After all, I thought that you were a footman — nobody ever looks very closely at a footman; and the light was poor, and your voice was disguised, and I am only a sweet, innocent, naturally unsuspicious young creature. Dick won't believe a word of it, of course, but dear Dick will have to hold his tongue in public — though I fancy he's going to express himself rather fluently in private."

"Why did you stop to gaze at the jail whenever you went over to Goshen?"

"I told Christopher to bring the horse around to that big elm at the first turn of the drive. He ought to be there by this time. Suppose you put this bread and cheese in your pocket and slip out quietly through the window? This dance will be over in another moment now — and they'll look for me if I'm not in the room."

"Who always gets what he wants, Barbara?"

"Are you going, Captain Sherwood?"

"The instant you answer my question, Miss Grahame. Who always gets what he wants, Barbara?"

"Peaceable, please! I can't discuss this with you now — later — some other time — when the war's over — "

"Who always gets what he wants, Barbara?" I asked again, and held out both my hands to her.

"You do," said Barbara helplessly, and put hers into them.

"When the war's over, dearest?"

"When the war's over, dearest," she promised gravely.

There was no time to say anything else. The music from the outer room swept up to the end of the dance, and then died away in a rustle of skirts and ripple of conversation as the dancers scattered. I swung myself up to the low window sill, turned to drop down into the garden, paused suddenly, and glanced back.

"Do you remember Dick's asking what I came to bring you?" I demanded.

"Yes, of course, but — "

211

"It wouldn't do to disappoint Dick, would it?" I felt in the pocket of my coat for the signet ring I had put there, found it, leaned forward, and dropped it into her hand. "Keep that for me until I can get back with the real one," I said, and went away.

"And you got to New York safely?" I asked eagerly.

"Yes, without the slightest —" Peaceable Sherwood broke off abruptly and turned his head as if to listen.

"Someone's coming," he murmured, and disappeared from view around the corner of the screen just as a young man in evening dress opened the door of the butler's pantry and made his way along the wall toward the corner with the punch bowl. For an instant I thought it must be one of the waiters coming back for my plate of chicken salad; then I recognized him, and fell back weakly in my chair with a little gasp.

"Pat, you fool!" I whispered. "How on earth did you ever get in here?"

"Through the pantry window," replied Pat, with a modest smile, as if he had done something clever. "I said I was going to dance with you before the night had ended, didn't I?"

"Dance!" I repeated sarcastically. "You dance yourself straight back through that pantry window before Uncle Enos finds out you're here, and —"

A voice from the other side of the screen interrupted me. It was a high, imperious old lady's voice, very distinct above the low laughter and the music.

"Enos! Enos! One moment, if you please! I've been looking for you. What's all this I hear about your adopting poor Ricky's daughter? Where is the child? Why isn't she dancing? Didn't she come tonight? I haven't even met her yet."

A second and deeper voice rumbled something in reply. The speakers must have been standing just around the edge of the screen. Nobody could go down to the pantry now without running straight into them.

"Uncle Enos?" inquired Pat, cocking his head.

"Uncle Enos," I answered shakily.

Pat perched himself on one corner of the table and stole an olive from my chicken salad. "Well, anyway, it's been nice knowing you," he remarked philosophically.

"Stand up!" I hissed. "Stand up and turn your back and pretend you're collecting those empty cups on a tray. They may think you're just one of the waiters. Quick, you lunatic! It's our only chance!" — and I rose curtseying to my feet in all my flowered satin as Uncle Enos and his companion appeared around the corner of the screen.

"Mrs. Cunningham, may I present my niece?" asked Uncle Enos formally. "Richard's daughter, Peggy."

213

Mrs. Cunningham was an old, old lady in black velvet and diamonds, with a sharp, wicked, mischievous face that looked remarkably like the Bad Fairy in one of my nursery books. Her diamonds glittered just as they had in the picture, and she was carrying exactly the same sort of tall ebony cane with a circle of silver around the handle. The end of the cane swished a trifle from time to time rather as if it were the tip of a cat's tail.

"Would either of you care for a little punch?" I quavered politely.

"Not if it's more of that authentic eighteenth-century stuff Enos was serving last year," said old Mrs. Cunningham with the utmost frankness. "You're a pretty child to be one of the Grahames, I must say. What are you doing shut away here in this ridiculous corner all by yourself? Some of your uncle's nonsense, I suppose. You ought to be out enjoying yourself with the other young people. And that reminds me — Enos! Is the Thorne boy anywhere about? I promised Helen Arlington I'd look him up when I was in London last spring. Dr. Lewis tells me he's over at New Jerusalem boarding at Susan Dykemann's while he does some sort of research. Isn't he here? I want to ask him to tea."

"I don't know him," said Uncle Enos, in his most forbidding voice.

Old Mrs. Cunningham merely rapped the ebony cane on the floor.

214

"Nonsense!" she said sharply. "You ought to keep up the connection."

I heard Uncle Enos draw a hard, passionate breath. But he could not very well tell old Mrs. Cunningham to go to her room, for she had no room at Rest-and-be-thankful, nor yet to run along like a good child and stop bothering him either.

"I must say I'm surprised at you, Enos," she went on, surveying the leading historian of Orange County as if he were a particularly tiresome small boy. "Boarding at Susan Dykemann's, indeed! Your poor grandfather must be turning over in his grave."

"I should have invited him to stay at Rest-and-be-thankful, no doubt?" Uncle Enos's tone would have frozen most people to the marrow, but it seemed to have no effect on old Mrs. Cunningham whatever.

"And why not?" she snapped impatiently. "That cousin of his — Mildred What's-her-name — had you down for the weekend when you went over to England last winter, didn't she? After the old gentleman died? I should think it would be the least you could do in return. Of course, Helen Arlington says that Mildred What's-her-name has been getting more and more peculiar for the last year or so; but the boy is perfectly presentable by all accounts — and at any rate he seems to be trying to earn his own living, which is more than you can say for most of that family." Somewhere behind me there was a sudden choking, strangling sound and a tremendous rattle of glass.

"Be careful of those cups, young man!" said old Mrs. Cunningham briskly. "Well, Enos? And don't try to play off any of your fine-gentlemanly airs on me! I know you! What's the meaning of all this?"

Uncle Enos had begun to look slightly unsteady, like a man trying to keep his feet in a high wind.

"There really can't be any question of my entertaining anybody just now," he mumbled. "I've been very busy with my article for *Antiques and Collectors,* and the fact is I've not been feeling particularly well for the last month or —"

"Of course you haven't been feeling well! You always started running a temperature the minute you got into any sort of trouble. And don't talk fiddle-faddle to me about being busy! Selfish and inconsiderate is what you mean. You've never had the smallest regard for anything except your own convenience since the day you were born. Look at this poor child here!"

"What poor child?" asked Uncle Enos hazily, taken completely unawares by this sudden change of attack.

"A fine time she seems to have had of it all evening!" said old Mrs. Cunningham, with another rap of the ebony cane. "You and your punch bowls and your traditions and your notions! Didn't it ever

216

occur to you that she might like a dance now and then along with the other girls? I declare, Enos, you are enough to try the patience of a saint! Be off with you and find her a partner at once! They'll be making up another set in a moment — I can hear the music now. Peggy, go tidy your hair. Those roses in it will be coming down altogether the next time you try to curtsey. And tell that waiter to take those absurd cups away to the pantry before he drops the rest of them!"

And without waiting for an answer from any of us, she turned and was gone, her cane rapping on the floor and Uncle Enos trailing helplessly behind her. I could hear her imperious voice announcing, "No, Enos, I don't want to go back to the library; there's still a good deal I have to say to you," as the rapping died away. Pat had collapsed over the table with the cups on it, his head in his hands and his shoulders heaving and shaking uncontrollably with laughter.

"Will you be quiet!" I begged. "Do you want everybody in the house to hear you?"

"I d-don't care," sobbed Pat. "L-let them find me. Let them take me away to the Goshen jail. It was worth it. Wasn't she superb? Of all the perishing old marvels! Be careful of those cups, young man! Which is more than can be said for most of that family! And the look on your Uncle Enos's face when she told him not to talk fiddle-faddle to her!"

"You're coming back to the butler's pantry this instant."

"Peggy, go tidy your hair."

"This instant," I said firmly.

"But what was all that about your Uncle Enos keeping up the connection?" Pat demanded. "I knew there was a connection, of course, but I never thought it amounted to anything much."

"Oh, do please come along, Pat! I haven't the faintest idea."

"And all that about Cousin Mildred asking him down for the weekend when he was in England last winter?" Pat went on, following me along the wall and in at the pantry door. He had stopped laughing now and his voice sounded puzzled and a little distressed. "I didn't even know your Uncle Enos had gone to England. My Cousin Mildred certainly never breathed a word about it to me."

"I don't know, I tell you! And for heaven's sake, don't stand there worrying about it now! Just be an angel and go away quietly, won't you? I can't possibly stay. She may start looking for me again if I'm not in the room."

"She'd probably only tell me not to fall into the flower bed and crush all the day lilies," said Pat, swinging himself up on the low window sill. He turned to drop into the garden, paused suddenly, and glanced back.

"You're a perishing marvel yourself, you know, Peggy," he said softly. "I like to see you dealing with a crisis. That notion about the waiter would never have occurred to me. Whatever made you think of it so quickly?"

"You'd be surprised," I informed him.

The Secrets

I WAS CURLED UP miserably on the south window seat in the library, trying to read a book I had found on one of the back shelves. It was a very old book, bound in musty calf with ornate brass clasps holding it together at the corners. It had been published in London in 1616. I had taken it down because I was attracted by the title: *A Treatise of Apparitions and Spirits Walking the Earth,* by "that Learned and Excellent Minister of the Gospel, Doctor Abraham Potter." Facing the title page was an engraved portait of the author himself, wearing a large ruff and a small black skullcap, his quill pen poised over a sheet of paper and his eyes lifted to heaven as if waiting for the spirits and apparitions to come down and inspire him.

The learned and excellent Doctor Potter had gone into his subject very thoroughly. The first chapter consisted of a long dissertation on the nature of spirits and apparitions in general, with a great many quotations in Latin and Greek from the Bible, the classics, the Fathers of the Church, and a number of Renaissance authorities whose very names were unfamiliar to me. The following chapter took up the question: "Whether and upon what Occasions the Spirits of the Dead may be Verily Asserted to Revisit Those yet Living." These spirits all seemed to be quite different from the sort to which I had become accustomed at Rest-and-be-thankful. There were ghosts who could not rest because they had been secretly murdered — ghosts who were trying to reveal where they had hidden some treasure — ghosts who rose to warn their country's leaders of some approaching revolution or catastrophe — false ghosts who were actually devils in disguise — ghosts who . . . ghosts who . . .

It was no use. I could not concentrate. Try as I might, I kept turning my head every minute or so to look down the drive for some sign of the doctor's car. The doctor had already called once at Rest-and-be-thankful during the morning, but he had said something just before he left about dropping in again on his way back to New Jerusalem when he had finished his afternoon round.

Uncle Enos was very sick.

Poor Uncle Enos! After doing his best to live like a fine old traditional eighteenth-century gentleman all his life, he had at last come down with a fine old traditional disease — the sort of thing which eighteenth-century novelists would have described as a wasting fever. Dr. Lewis had talked very impressively about the possibility of a virus infection complicated by fatigue and overexertion, but that made no difference. It still looked like a plain case of wasting fever to me.

At first I had thought that he was only worn out after all the excitement of the Independence Day Ball. He had somehow managed to drag himself downstairs the following morning, and we had all been so tired and so busy with the cleaning-up ourselves that we did not pay very much attention to him. The next morning he did not come to breakfast; and when Christopher Seven went up to call him, his room was empty and the bed had not been slept in. I finally found him in his study, at the desk with his head down on a pile of scattered papers, where he had apparently been sitting ever since the night before.

Even then he had stubbornly refused to let us send for the doctor and had shut himself up in his own room for the rest of the day, insisting that he would be perfectly all right if we would only have the sense to leave him alone. The day afterwards he was too ill to protest when I called in the doctor on my own responsibility.

By the time he came Uncle Enos was running a very high temperature and had begun to toss restlessly about in the big four-poster bed. Nothing that the doctor was able to do seemed to help very much. The fever would not go down, and even sedatives apparently had little or no effect on the restlessness. He could not sleep, and he could not eat, and he could not seem to remain quiet for an instant. He hardly ever spoke, and — this terrified me more than anything else — he never uttered a word of complaint. He only lay there growing weaker every hour and tossing continually as if he were trying to struggle free from some invisible weight that was smothering him.

"Do you happen to know if there's anything weighing on his mind, Miss Grahame?" said the doctor rather anxiously at the end of the first week. "Of course, virus infections can do very odd things sometimes, and your uncle has never been what I'd call a good patient, but he ought to be responding to treatment more than he is. I'm beginning to think that at least part of the trouble must be nervous tension. Has he had any particular difficulty worrying him lately? I don't mean just the Independence Day Ball — but something really serious?"

I could only shake my head. "He never told me anything at all about himself," I admitted wretchedly. "Only to run along and stop bothering him sometimes. He hated anything that looked like curiosity or meddling or interfering with his private business."

"Well, whatever it is, he ought to get it off his mind and be done with it," said the doctor. "He

can't go on like this much longer. If he'd only relax and let the sedative take hold, he might have a
chance. If he'd even give in and tell me what's
worrying him, we might be able to do something
about it. But you might just as well argue with a
stone wall."

"There's old Mrs. Cunningham," I suggested
tentatively. "Do you think it would do any good to
ask her? She took him off to the library to talk to
him about something the night of the Independence
Day Ball. Maybe she was the one who upset him."

But old Mrs. Cunningham, sweeping up to the
door in an incredible Rolls-Royce only one step
removed from a coach, could do little except repeat
what the doctor had already said in her own words,
which were considerably more picturesque but
equally unhelpful.

"Of course Enos has been up to mischief, that's
perfectly obvious," she remarked, rapping her cane
and looking more like the Bad Fairy than ever. "He
broke my silver lustre cream pitcher when he was
a boy, and hid the pieces, and then went home and
was sick in bed for a week. I don't mean that he was
a cowardly child who couldn't stand the idea of a
whipping. It was just that he always took the most
absurdly lofty view of himself, and when he was
tripped up by the devil like anybody else, he simply
couldn't bear to admit it. The trouble was, he
couldn't live with himself afterwards either. Your

224

dear father was the only Grahame I ever met who
didn't have a tendency to suffer from ingrown conscience anyway" — she spoke as if a conscience were
a particularly inconvenient form of toenail — "but
Enos always seemed to get it especially hard whenever he got it at all. He ran his temperature up to
a hundred and five that time before I found the
pieces where he'd buried them under the Rose-of-
Sharon in the shrubbery . . . No, I can't tell you
what's the matter with him now. That born fool
Alison Douglas came rushing up to us in the dining
room before I could get it out of him. I suppose he
must have been sickening with it for a long time,
and then this virus infection coming on top of everything else brought him down with a crash. It's
something to do with the Thorne boy, of course.
Why don't you come over on Sunday and see what
he knows about it? I've sent him a note inviting him
to tea at five if that ridiculous Ford of Ted Lowry's
will hold together till then."

There was no way I could tell old Mrs. Cunningham that Pat knew nothing whatever and could not
possibly be of any help to us, and I felt bereft of my
last hope as I thanked her for her kindness and
watched the Rolls-Royce go creaking majestically
off down the drive. It had already occurred to me
that the "particular difficulty" worrying Uncle Enos
was tied up somehow with his treatment of Pat. I
could still remember only too clearly how he had

225

collapsed in his chair that first afternoon whispering, "What shall I do now? What on earth shall I do?" and the white, drawn, miserable look on his face. But it did no good to feel certain about the cause of the trouble as long as I could not discover what the trouble itself was. Asking Uncle Enos point-blank in his present condition would have been perfectly useless and would only have made matters worse. All I could do was try to find out for myself — and so far I had completely failed to think of anything which poor, dear, fantastic, maddening Uncle Enos could conceivably have on his conscience. And meanwhile he went on tossing feverishly upstairs on the same big four-poster bed where the haughty, suffering little boy had once lain and also tossed because he could not live with himself any longer, and nobody could find the broken bits of silver lustre he had carried away and hidden in the shrubbery.

"Maybe it will come to me if I just don't keep worrying at it so hard," I whispered to myself, smoothing a few tear splashes off the musty pages of Abraham Potter and doing my best to concentrate my attention on him again. There was nothing else I could do. Dr. Lewis was trying a new sedative to make Uncle Enos sleep, and had ordered us all to keep out of his room. Christopher Seven was sitting outside the door in the hall upstairs.

"And there be some scholars," I made myself read on:

— some scholars (and among them men eminent
for their wisdom and holiness) who maintain
that there are yet another sort of spirits who may
return to the earth: and these not to uncover
secret murder, nor yet to reveal hidden treasure,
nor yet for any purpose hitherto set down — but
rather out of pure charity to give what help and
comfort they may to such of their descendants
who continue to dwell in the same house.

I straightened up and began to read more carefully. Abraham Potter was becoming interesting at
last.

True it is, that the ingenious Johannes Calo-
vius argues very learnedly that this is but a notion or fantastical opinion drawn out from those
fables of attendant spirits which the heathen
relate, or the guardian angels concerning which
the Papists fondly dispute. Yet for myself I
rather believe that such visitations do verily
occur, though indeed (as I allow) they must
needs happen but seldom, and this for the following reason, viz. to wit: that these spirits do
never show themselves except to young maidens
who are sorely neglected by their own kin, and
more especially to those who are so unfortunate
that they have never in all their days received
from them the smallest caress or token of favor:
no, not so much as a kiss from their own fathers

and mothers, Wherefore (it is said) the shades of their family are permitted by the merciful providence of God to do what they can to cheer them in their need: and that need being satisfied, they depart away again and are seen no more.

"Well, Peggy," said a familiar voice on the other side of the room, "is it any clearer to you now?"

Barbara Grahame had come back again and was standing over by the study, with one hand on the knob of the door. She looked a little older than she did the last time I had seen her. She was no longer wearing the crimson riding cloak, but instead a soft flowing dress of deep rose that shimmered delicately as it caught the light. She had a locket or something of the sort on a thin fine chain around her neck, but I could not see exactly what it was because it had slipped in under the lace ruffles at the edge of her bodice.

"Yes, it's all clear, but — oh, I am so glad to see you! You don't know how I've needed you. Uncle Enos is sick, and we can't find out what he's got on his mind, and I wondered if you could possibly tell me —"

But Barbara Grahame was shaking her head.

"No, my dear," she said gently but very decidedly. "That you must work out for yourself."

"But you can stay with me a little while, anyway?"

228

I begged. "You won't go, will you? Everything's so horrible, and I haven't got anybody else."

Barbara Grahame gave a soft, half rueful little laugh. Her eyes had the same amused, secret look which Copley had caught in the portrait. "No, I won't go," she said. "Don't you remember? It's only when your need is satisfied that I — how did he put it? — depart away again and am seen no more."

"Why is it that I see you more than any of the others?" I asked curiously. "This is the third time now. Dick and Eleanor and Peaceable have only come once."

Barbara Grahame laughed again. "I suppose it's really because we're both so much alike," she answered. "The difficulties we seem to get into with young men from England!"

"Oh, but that isn't the same at all," I objected hurriedly. "Not in the least. There's never been the remotest question of my marrying Pat."

"I remember saying something of the sort myself about Peaceable."

"But did you really marry him in the end?"

Peaceable usually got what he wanted (said Barbara Grahame), even when it was a matter of waiting a long time for it. And it *was* a long time, too. He had gone back to his own army, of course, and the fighting dragged on and on, and there was never any chance of even hearing from him. I once met some-

229

body who thought he'd had a glimpse of him during a skirmish somewhere in the South, but that was the only word I had. It couldn't actually have been more than three years altogether, I suppose, counting from Christmas to Christmas, but they seemed more like centuries — and when Dick came up from New York that night in December and said the peace treaty was signed at last, it was a moment before I could bring myself to believe it.

"But it's true, I tell you!" Dick insisted. "I heard it from a man who was just off the first ship from London with the news. They were ringing every bell in the city last night before I left. The war's really over. You can take that preposterous ring off that chain under your bodice where you fondly suppose you've been concealing it all these years, and put it on your finger if you like."

"What ring are you talking about?"

"Oh, my dear sister!" Dick retorted. "I may be ninety-seven years old and falling more into decay with every hour, but I was young myself once, and somewhere a faint gleam of intelligence still flickers among the ashes." He pulled me to my feet and kissed me affectionately. "Don't look so white, Barbara! The war's really over at last — and I wish you joy with all my heart. I even brought you a bride gift all the way from New York to mark the occasion. You'll find it waiting for you downstairs in the treasure room."

I gave my brother a quick, suspicious glance, and Dick gazed innocently back at me, looking as solemn as a bishop. But it was a good many years since I had believed every word he said, or had sat on the edge of my chair trying to "smell the misery" at Aunt Susanna's house in New Jerusalem. I knew better than to trust him now. The treasure room had always been our name for a large hidden closet off the study which old Enos Grahame had built as a hiding place for the family valuables. I could think of no reason why Dick should have brought me a present from New York and put it away down there.

"You might at least say thank you," he remarked, in a deeply injured voice. "Why don't you just run along downstairs and see what it is before I begin to imagine that you don't really appreciate me? I've got to wash off this dust and go break the news to Father and Eleanor."

I went downstairs prepared for anything, from a live frog in a bracelet box to the whole family lined up on the hearth rug singing "Haste to the Wedding" in chorus as I entered the study. But the study was quite empty and silent, with a bright fire burning briskly in the grate. The door of the treasure room was not even ajar as it had been on one occasion many years before when Dick had put a cold-water pitcher at the top to catch me as I went in. I pressed the secret spring on the carving and paused cautiously just across the threshold.

A tall and very elegantly dressed young man in a fawn-colored driving cloak was standing with his back to me, apparently absorbed in examining the inlay of the cabinet on the other side of the room.

"I beg your pardon, Miss Grahame," he murmured apologetically, without so much as turning his head. "I'm afraid this is your brother's idea of a joke. But I met him by chance as I was landing from my ship, and he was so kind about bringing me here at once that I couldn't very well refuse to let him do it in his own way. I had thought I might have to fetch you down a ladder in the middle of the night and carry you off on my saddlebow while Dick and your father pursued us over the border with whip and spur like the Grahames and Sherwoods in the Middle Ages. By the by, do you still have that ring of mine that I left with you?"

I held the ring out to him dumbly, quite unable to speak, and he turned around and took first the hand with the ring in it and then the other in both his own.

"We were standing in approximately this position, as I remember it," he went on, "and what was it you were saying to me just before we were interrupted?"

"I was saying that I might talk to you again when the war was over."

" ' — when the war was over, dearest,' " Peaceable corrected me. "Now, suppose we go on from there."

232

We went on from there so long that it must have been almost an hour before we finally came out and found Dick and Eleanor and my father all drinking sherry around the fire in the study.

"What I don't understand, Richard," my father was saying as I opened the door, "is why Barbara should have taken him off to the treasure room."

"That is a little puzzling, sir," Dick agreed politely, lifting his glass to us across my father's shoulder. "You'll have to ask Barbara. Perhaps she thought he was valuable."

"The treasure room has always been such a secret in the family."

"I expect it's still in the family," said Dick.

Barbara Grahame stopped speaking abruptly, and I saw the knob of the study door turn a little under her hand as if she were about to open it and go back.

"But what happened then?" I demanded eagerly.

"Hush!" said Barbara Grahame. "Listen!"

Somewhere overhead there was a sudden wild rattle of feet over the floor, and then Christopher Seven's voice calling frantically, "Miss Peggy! Miss Peggy! Where is you? Come here, Miss Peggy!"

I never saw what happened to Barbara Grahame. I sprang from the window seat, tumbling poor Abraham Potter off my knee, and went flying up the stairs three steps at a time, with my heart in my throat.

The hall at the head of the stairs was empty, and the door of the room just beyond flung back against the wall. Christopher Seven was over by the four-poster bed.

Uncle Enos was trying to get up. The new sedative had not put him to sleep yet — it had only knocked him off his feet; and he was still semi-conscious and talking in a thick, drugged jumble of words. Christopher Seven had him by the shoulders, but he could not seem to hold him. He went on struggling with both of us for another moment; then his strength gave out and he fell back against the pillows, his eyes almost shut and his breath coming in slow, painful gasps.

"I have to — go — downstairs," he panted. "I — have to — get —" He made another desperate effort to rise.

"What is it?" I begged him. "What is it that you want, Uncle Enos? Tell me and I'll bring it to you, and then you can go to sleep."

Uncle Enos's hands went out in a strange groping gesture, as if he thought I was going to put something into them. "Where are they?" he muttered. "I want . . . I can't . . . Didn't — you — find them?"

"No, not yet, but I will," I answered reassuringly. "I promise you that I will. Truly I will, if you'll just lie quietly and rest a little while."

One of the groping hands caught my wrist and closed hard around it.

234

"You promise?" Uncle Enos whispered.

"I promise," I repeated gently. "Just tell me what it is that you want, dear."

"I . . . want . . ." but the voice was becoming only an incoherent murmur and I could no longer understand what he was saying. I caught the name "Peggy," and then the words "own" and "paneling" and "book," and then another name that sounded like "Earle," and then — very rapidly and urgently — something about "history" and "papers" and "Earle" again.

"Christopher Seven, who is it that he's talking about?" I demanded.

"I don't know, Miss Peggy," said Christopher Seven helplessly.

Uncle Enos's hand fell away from my wrist and began to move restlessly about once more, trying to find and close over something that was not there.

"Where . . . I . . . must . . . can't . . . any longer," he muttered; and then, in a high, sharp, distinct voice: "Peggy!"

"Yes, dear?"

"Thorne," said Uncle Enos. "Thorne."

"What's that you after now, Mr. Enos?" quavered Christopher Seven.

"Peggy," repeated Uncle Enos. "Thorne."

I bent down over the bed.

"Uncle Enos, is it Pat Thorne you want?" I asked as clearly as I could.

Uncle Enos's eyes opened for an instant and looked up into mine, then they closed again and the hands resumed their feverish wandering over the coverlet. But he seemed to be lying a little more quietly. The desperate jumble of words stopped, and his head turned over on the pillow with a long gasping sigh.

"You stay with him till the doctor gets here," I called over my shoulder to Christopher Seven as I swung around and made for the door as fast as my feet would carry me. "Tell him I've gone to fetch whatever it is if he starts talking again! I'll be back just as soon as I can." And then I was dashing down the stairs and through the hall and out the side porch into the garden.

There was only one telephone at Rest-and-be-thankful — and that was far away across the orchard at the gardener's cottage in Mrs. MacIntosh's back pantry, where Uncle Enos was officially supposed to be unaware of its existence. Fortunately, Mrs. MacIntosh was a kindhearted woman and had simply set a painted china piggy bank on the pantry shelf along with the memorandum pad and the telephone book, as a gentle reminder to all of us that we were expected to drop in a contribution to the monthly bill.

"No, I don't care, Miss Peggy," she had said the first time I had met her, "though I must say it's a blessing that your dear grandmother managed to get the bathrooms put in at the big house before your Uncle Enos could come along with any more of his quirks and his notions. Yes, you go right ahead and use the phone whenever you like. I don't care a bit. It gives me a chance to see a little company."

She might have added, "— and hear all the gossip," for her ears were as sharp as her heart was kind, and poor Petunia had almost given up trying to have a quiet word of an evening with the new janitor who worked at the Methodist Church. The emergency calls and crises and excitement of a serious illness in the family were exactly the sort of thing Mrs. MacIntosh liked best, and she was throbbing at the kitchen door that afternoon before I could even turn in to the path.

"Miss Peggy, oh dear, what's the matter?" she cried as she caught sight of my face. "Why, you must have run all the way from the house! Is he worse?"

"No, but would you mind if I used the telephone? I have to call somebody at New Jerusalem," I panted, fumbling through the directory for Mrs. Dykemann's number and praying frantically that Pat would not be out somewhere in Betsy or over at Goshen for a day in the library. I could have cried with relief when I heard the receiver click and then the voice saying at the other end of the line: "Hullo? I'm sorry; Mrs. Dykemann's not in."

"No, not Mrs. Dykemann, you," I gasped. "Pat, it's Peggy. Can you come over to Rest-and-be-thank-

ful? Yes, that was what I said. Now? Right away?
Uncle Enos wants to see you."

"Good heavens! Has he gone out of his mind?"

"Something like that, and — oh, please will you
hurry? I'm afraid it's most awfully urgent."

"Hang on, I'm coming," replied Pat briefly, and
I heard the receiver go down again.

"Now, you'll just sit right down here at this table
and have a good hot cup of tea and a cookie," announced Mrs. MacIntosh, bustling about sympa-
thetically somewhere behind me. "I always say
there's nothing like a good hot cup of tea when
you're feeling a little low. That's the young man
who's boarding over at Susan Dykemann's, isn't it?"

"I've got to go up to the gate and meet him, Mrs.
MacIntosh; thank you anyway."

"He can't possibly be there for another half hour
at the very least, not in that Ford of Ted Lowry's,"
said Mrs. MacIntosh cajolingly. "I baked the cookies myself this morning. Just you try one, they're
nice and fresh. Did you meet him somewhere
abroad? Susan Dykemann doesn't know what to
make of him. She says his socks are worn out till you
can hardly see them for the holes, but all his hair
brushes are real solid silver."

I finally escaped by taking two of the fresh-baked
cookies with me and promising faithfully that I
would eat them while I waited for Pat by the gate.
It was a heavenly summer day, high and warm and

blue, and all the trees in the orchard were already crowded thick with little green apples. I stood leaning on the fence and counted the knotholes on one of the posts mechanically over and over again, trying desperately not to cry. I had never in all my life felt quite so cold or miserable or sick.

Then Betsy suddenly charged out of the woods at the edge of the hill, her convertible top pulled grimly over the windshield like a jockey's cap and her wheels sending up showers of pebbles as she tore down the slope and collapsed with a triumphant puff in the long grass at the side of the road. Pat came out of the seat and across the gate in what appeared to be a single swift movement, and caught me as I ran stumbling to meet him.

"My poor lamb, what on earth is the matter?" he demanded, with his arm around me.

I had kept control of myself fairly well up to that point, but the words and the touch made me go completely to pieces. I put my head down on his shoulder without even knowing I had done it, and clung to him weeping helplessly while I tried incoherently to tell him everything between my sobs. Pat listened with a little frown of concentration, one hand smoothing my arm absent-mindedly and his eyes looking over my head at the house in the distance.

"And you're certain I'm the one he wants to see?" he asked, adding in a bracing manner that I had better fish around in the left-hand pocket of his coat

239

for a handkerchief and see if I couldn't stop crying for a bit.

I took the handkerchief, which had apparently been used to dry Betsy's tears too sometime already that day, and mopped my face gratefully with a clean corner. "He said your name over and over again, and then when I asked him he seemed to understand and get a little quieter," I answered shakily. "There's somebody else called Earle that he wants besides, but I don't know who he is. Christopher Seven says he never heard of him."

"That's all right, it isn't important. Don't worry about it any more — Not that handkerchief, you idiot! I've been using it to wipe down the windscreen. This one!"

"But Pat, you don't understand! It must be important. The way he kept talking — "

"It's all right, I tell you. He was probably only trying to say something else about me."

"But your name isn't Earle, or anything like it! And it was 'Earle' he was saying, I'm perfectly sure of that."

"Of course my name isn't Earle!" snapped Pat, looking rather embarrassed and completely exasperated. "It isn't even Thorne, either, if it comes to that. The family name is something quite different. Thorne's only the title."

I pulled myself out of his arm and took a step backwards, staring up dumbfounded into his face.

"Pat, are you an *earl?*" I demanded incredulously.

"Oh heaven give me patience!" moaned Pat. "You've been reading old books again. What do you expect an earl to look like? Want to see me ride up to the gate on my coal-black hunter followed by my pack of hounds and my personal string of faithful retainers? You little know modern England! There hasn't been a whole loaf of bread at Thorne since about the time of the Boer War, and even the death-duty and income-tax people are beginning to get tired of nosing about the place for crumbs. We'll probably have to spend the rest of our lives in some deplorable flat on a dusty street behind a red brick university where I teach history for a pittance; and it will be a serious question whether it's more important to buy Meg her new umbrella or get the blazer for Johnny, because we'll never be able to afford them both at once; and some time if you'd like to see the family estate we'll pack a picnic hamper and go down on the cheap excursion train for the day along with the other tourists; and oh yes, you'd better learn how to make bread sauce, because they tell me it makes the Sunday chicken stretch a little further — and now do you understand what it's really going to be like when we're married?"

"When we're . . . what?"

"Married," said Pat, casually. "Don't look so taken aback! Surely it can't really be news to you? I've had it in my mind ever since I saw you standing

241

there in the road with your shoes all over mud."

"B-but —"

"And don't bother trying to argue with me about it. You can have as long as you like to accustom yourself to the idea, but you may as well get it through your head now that nothing you can do will make the slightest difference in the end. The members of my family have always been as stubborn as mules, and notoriously good at getting what they wanted. We even have a motto about it on our coat of arms: *quod desidero obtineo,* which, roughly translated, means —"

My whole universe suddenly seemed to splinter and crack and go whirling chaotically in bits around my head like the pieces of a gigantic jigsaw puzzle.

"Pat! Wait a minute! No, please listen to me! What did you say your family name was? Not the Thorne part — the other?"

"Sherwood," said Pat, looking rather bewildered. "What's the matter? Did you expect it to be something like Montmorency or Plantagenet? Peggy Plantagenet would be a horrible name."

"And your ancestor you were telling me about — you know, the eighteenth-century Thorne who was with the British Army in New York — was he called Sherwood too? Peaceable Drummond Sherwood?"

"That was the one. He didn't come into the title and so on till after the war. I believe he was originally a nephew or something of the sort."

242

"And he was the man with the diary and the letters and all the other stuff you couldn't find any trace of?"

"Yes."

"And the diary — was it written in a brown leather book with his coat of arms on the cover?"

Pat frowned suddenly. "Yes; I remember now — there were about nine or ten of them altogether. But how on earth did you — ?"

I drew a deep breath. Great fragments of the jigsaw puzzle were beginning to fall into place and fit together at last.

"Pat, I'm afraid I know what's become of your things. Uncle Enos must have them."

"What?"

"I'm not sure about the rest, but he had one of the diary books in his study last month. I saw it accidentally when I was trying to pick up his notes for him after the big thunderstorm. I expect he's got all the others put away somewhere too."

"But that just isn't possible! Where in the world could your Uncle Enos have —" Pat broke off abruptly, his face clearing. "Of course! It must have been at that weekend in the country with Cousin Mildred after the old gentleman died. The one Mrs. Cunningham was talking about at the party." He leaned back against the gate and began to laugh helplessly. "Oh, naughty Uncle Enos! Do you suppose he carried them off down a ladder and smuggled them aboard the lugger in the middle of the night?"

"But I thought you said your Cousin Mildred told you that she'd never heard of them, and she'd hung a picture of Salisbury Cathedral over the place where the miniature used to be, and I don't see any reason why she should do that unless she — she —" My voice faltered and went to pieces. I could not think of any tactful way to finish the sentence.

"That's right," said Pat approvingly. "A courteous reticence in speaking about your husband's family is the key to a successful married life. But if you would like to ask: is my Cousin Mildred the sort of person who would sell those papers without consulting me and then try to carry the matter off with a high hand afterwards? the answer is: yes, I'm afraid so. In fact, I ought to have thought of it myself. She's an old lady, you see, and she's lived at the place all her life, and I suppose she's just gotten into the way of thinking about everything in it as more or less belonging to her. I don't mean she would have made off with the pearls or anything else she really regarded as valuable family property. But a box of dirty old papers that had been lying around the library for years on end without anyone paying the slightest attention to them? It wouldn't strike her as being the same sort of thing at all. And then when I charged in asking questions and pulling the house apart trying to find where they were — of course, she flew into a panic. You can't blame her."

"But Uncle Enos! He must have known."

"Not necessarily at the time he bought them. I fancy she wrote to him after her balloon got off the string. And then he flew into a panic too."

"But he couldn't have! Why should he?"

"I know the answer to that one." Pat's mouth twisted wryly, and for an instant there was a curious, self-questioning look in his eyes. "It's the good old occupational disease I always think of as the Scholar's Clutch. Don't you realize the Sherwood Papers are probably going to be the biggest historical discovery in their own field for a generation at least? I tell you that he could no more have given them up once he had his hands on them than — well, than I might have been able to if I'd been in his place. You think about it a minute. There he was, with his pen practically dipped in the ink to start rewriting the whole history of Orange County and New York and the War of Independence — and then he suddenly finds out that he doesn't have any valid claim to the material, and it all really belongs to some young whippersnapper with no reputation as a scholar who might make a complete botch of the job!"

"That isn't any excuse."

"No, I suppose not. There can't be very much wrong with him, though. He could perfectly well have blackmailed me into holding my tongue by threatening to take the whole business into court and raise a scandal about poor Cousin Mildred. That doesn't seem even to have occurred to him. All he's tried to do is get rid of the problem by ignoring it in a grand manner."

" 'Run along and don't bother me!' " I said, laughing in spite of myself.

"Something like that. I rather think he must have done it on the spur of the moment to begin with, and then found that he'd landed himself in a completely impossible situation. He couldn't very well admit what had happened, and he couldn't publish the papers without everybody finding out, and as a good historian it must have broken his heart to keep them a secret, and he never knew when you or Mrs. Cunningham or somebody else might get on his track, and there I was at New Jerusalem like an innocent child playing hide-and-go-seek in the cellar where he'd hidden the body — and all in all, he's probably had a fine, merry time of it for the last month or so. I don't wonder he cracked up."

"And I didn't think there was anything he could possibly have on his conscience! Pat, it must be those papers he wants. He was trying to go downstairs to 'get' something this afternoon. And even after we put him back to bed, he went on groping about over the sheet and making me promise I'd 'find them.' Of course, and that's why he kept repeating your name the way he did. He was going to give them back to you."

"I said there couldn't be very much wrong with him. What do we do now? Go tell him that the game is up, but never mind, we're not playing for keeps?"

But when we got back to the house and halfway up the stairs, the doctor came out of the bedroom with his coat off, and told us to go away for another hour at least, and for heaven's sake to find those papers Uncle Enos seemed to have on his mind if we really wanted to make ourselves useful.

"Well, that ought not to take much doing, anyway," I remarked as I led the way down again. "They must be in the study some place. He wouldn't leave them anywhere else."

It seemed strange to be going through the study door again with Pat behind me, exactly as I had that first afternoon, and I could not help glancing across the room at the spot where Uncle Enos had stood with his arm stretched out while he ordered him to leave the house. Pat took no notice. He went straight across to the nearest bookcase and began examining the contents systematically one shelf at a time, pulling out a volume now and then to look at it more closely. I sat down on the floor by the big desk and tried the drawer where I had seen Uncle Enos lock away the diary on the afternoon of the thunderstorm. But the drawer was open now, and there was nothing in it except an untidy heap of catalogues from rare-book dealers, and some discarded notes for the article on the drinking customs of the eighteenth century.

The search took a long time. There were four bookcases in the room, tall ones set back at intervals between the panels of the wall, with brass-handled drawers to hold papers, built in under them. Uncle Enos had a bad habit of thrusting odd books away behind the regular rows, and Pat had to grope around at the back of all the shelves and then empty them out to make certain whenever his hand struck anything. The drawers underneath were a housekeeper's nightmare of manuscripts, off-prints, more discarded notes and catalogues, unframed engravings, manila folders full of correspondence, bundles of old bills tied up with tape, family records, files, bibliography cards, and historical documents of every sort and kind. Nowhere in the confusion was there any trace of the Sherwood Papers. At the end of an hour all we had found was the letter from Cousin Mildred, on eight sheets of airmail stationery in a very agitated hand, beginning: "Dear Mr. Grahame, I write in *great distress* to say that I am obliged to tell you —"

"Never mind the rest of it," said Pat. "We know all that. What on earth do you suppose he could have done with the stuff?"

I twisted one foot around the rung of the bookcase ladder as I sat perched on the top step, and gazed up at the tall shelves overhead. "Maybe he took the papers apart and slipped them one by one between the pages of the encyclopedia or something," I suggested.

"He might have if they'd only been a couple of brief notes written on tissue paper," retorted Pat. "Do use your head, Peggy! There must be enough of them to fill a packing case, and nine or ten diary books besides. That's not the sort of thing you can just tuck away into any odd corner and forget."

"No, I suppose not," I agreed dejectedly.

"In fact, I don't see how he can be keeping them in the study at all. We'd have found them by now. Where else might they be? Is there a safe somewhere in the house? Or any other place you use to hide away the family valuables?"

It was the word "valuables" that suddenly brought back to my mind something which I had completely forgotten in all the stress and excitement of the afternoon.

"Oh, good heavens!" I broke in. "Of course! Why didn't I think of that? He must have put them in the treasure room."

"What fancy names you do have for things," remarked Pat. "We call it the 'lock-up' at home in Thorne. Is the floor covered knee-deep with pirate's gold?"

"I haven't been inside. Uncle Enos never tells me anything, and I only heard about it by accident" — or was it really by accident? I wondered, remembering Barbara Grahame's voice and look when she had told me I would have to work things out for myself. "It's a big closet somewhere off the study, with a secret door."

Pat groaned. "It would be," he said briefly. "And how does one go about getting in? Do you know that too?"

"I'm afraid not. Just that it opens when you press a spring somewhere on the carving. Oh, dear!" I added, as my eyes went around the room.

The woodwork in the study was very modest — that is, compared to the big drawing room and the library, where the architect had really let himself go — but nobody could truthfully say that there wasn't a good deal of it. The four walls were sheathed in dark oak divided symmetrically into twelve long panels by the windows and the bookcases, the fireplace and the door. All the windows and bookcases curved over at the top into deep recessed fluted shells, and the curve of the shells was in turn taken up and echoed in reverse by garlands of carved fruit and flowers looped across the intervening panels — a different garland corresponding to each of the twelve months of the year, from roses and strawberries and ripe grass for June to ivy and berries and clusters of pine cones for December.

"I never realized before what a lot of curlicues and little knobby bits there are on these things," I remarked, frowning up at the December garland.

"Pat, this is going to take forever. I suppose we'll just have to start around the walls and press and rap and knock and beat till the door gives way."

Pat glanced back at me across the room, and for a moment there was something in his expression that made him look almost startlingly like Peaceable Sherwood. "My darling heart, we're not a pair of bumblebees on a window pane," he said gently. "Never run about exerting yourself unnecessarily when you can use your intelligence instead." He dropped down into the big wing chair and settled back comfortably with his hands linked around one knee. "Now! Before we start the pressing and rapping and knocking and beating, tell me one thing — did you say it was a large closet?"

"Yes, but —"

"Then it can't be just anywhere behind one of those panels — at least, not according to Lesson Two of my five-shilling course on How-To-Learn-Logic-By-Mail. A large closet has to have a large space to fit into. Very well. Turn over the page to Lesson Three. There are four walls in this room. Over on my left —" he waved his hand vaguely to the east, "the wall is made up of three panels separated by two windows opening on the garden. Kindly step to the nearest window and see if there's anything resembling a large closet jutting out on that side into the lilac bushes or the pansy bed."

"I can tell you without even looking. It's a perfectly straight wall. The flagstone path goes along there to the terrace."

"Very well. That leaves us with only the three remaining walls to worry about. The south wall facing me is made up of three panels separated by one bookcase and the door that leads into the library. As I remember it, the wall on the library side is also perfectly straight, and there's only the width of the doorway anywhere between the two rooms. Cross out the south wall. Very well. The north wall behind me is made up of three more panels separated by two bookcases. What's on the other side there?"

"It's the morning room where the ladies used to sit in the eighteenth century. I don't know whether there's a place for a closet on that side or not. We never use it nowadays."

"Be a lamb and run around through the hall and look it over while I plow through Lesson Four."

I ran around obediently and looked. There was no closet jutting out into the morning room, but neither was there any door through to the study. For a moment I wondered if there might not possibly be two walls, one false, with the treasure room lying the whole length between. But when I paced off the distance from the corner nearest the study to the first window, and then paced it off again on the path outside, I found that the distances matched, and that meant the partition could be only of normal thickness.

"I thought it would be," said Pat, with a sigh of satisfaction. "Cross out the north wall. Very well. Now we come to something really interesting. The west wall on my right is made up of three more panels separated by another bookcase and the fireplace. Just on the other side is the central hall stairway to the second floor. Is the space under the stairs open or closed in? I didn't notice."

"Closed. I was wondering just now why they didn't leave it open and put the door to the morning room there. I had to go all the way around at the back to get in."

"Hm'm. There must be room for the chimney in the thickness of the wall here too. A chimney and a closed flight of stairs in combination like this always rouses the blackest suspicion in anyone accustomed to ye olde Englishe manor houses where those ever-lasting Cavaliers and Roundheads and smugglers seemed to spend all their time chasing each other in and out of the paneling. I suppose at this point I ought to start tapping it to see if it sounds hollow somewhere, but I always think that must look so silly, like crawling around the rug with a magnifying glass — and if the man who designed that door knew his business, it won't sound hollow anyway." He got up stretching from the chair and stood facing the wall with his hands clasped lightly behind his back.

"Oh, do get on with it, Pat! Hurry!"

"The Sherwoods have always been a lazy lot. You

253

should hear some of the stories they tell about Peaceable Drummond. Give me a minute to think, can't you? Not, I think, that carved shell at the top of the bookcase. It's too high and inconveniently out of reach. These nice garlands on the panels look much more promising . . . The winter months for the fireside end of the room, what a pleasant idea. Starting at the left-hand corner nearest the library, we have November: oak leaves and apples and ears of dried corn. On the other side of the bookcase, December: ivy and berries and clusters of pine cones. And over here beyond the fireplace on the far right, just where the stairs in the hall must be getting high, we come to January: thorny briers and empty seed pods (br'rr, it's cold!) *and* tucked neatly away under the twist of ribbon that ties everything up — one single solitary summer daisy that doesn't belong there. Well, who'd have thought it? After he worked out all the others so carefully, too!"

"That's funny; I never noticed. Do you suppose he could have started carving the panel before he realized he was doing the wrong month?"

"Perhaps; but I don't believe it. To me it looked more like an eighteenth-century gentleman playing a mildly entertaining little joke on the general public. I think the time has come for that pressing and rapping and knocking and beating you were talking about. Now then! Ready? Sherwood the Magician puts his finger on the center of the daisy — the quickness of the hand deceives the eye — trumpet fanfare and roll of drums from the orchestra — all done by logic — and there you are!"

It really was almost like some act of magic. The dark January panel with the thorny briers and the empty seed pods turned sweetly and slid away in complete silence under Pat's hand, and the afternoon light flashed suddenly back blazing from crystal and silver and enamel and gold.

We were looking into a small paneled room that must have taken up the whole thickness of the chimney-wall and the raised space under the stairway beyond it. I had one dizzying glimpse of shelves covered with cups and medallions and coffers and candelabra and bowls — the Paul Revere punch bowl on a stand by itself — and a tall inlaid cabinet with narrow drawers that were apparently meant for jewels — and then I was down on the floor beside Pat, kneeling over a battered old chest, the lid thrown back and books and documents and letters spilling out of it in a great confused pile, along with an antique army sword, a signet ring, and a small miniature portrait in a round gold frame.

The next thing I remember clearly is sitting with one arm across the chest and staring down at the portrait in my hand. It must have been painted when he was still very young — perhaps sixteen or seventeen — but the smile was there already, and the air of elegance, and the lazy, mocking glint in the eyes. I put it down gently on my knee and picked up one of the papers. It was a letter to his uncle giving an extremely impertinent and hilariously funny account of his voyage to America on the troop ship, and ending: "I remain, with regret, your very undutiful and disobedient nephew to command, Peaceable Drummond Sherwood." I could not quite understand why Uncle Anthony had not thrown it into the fire the instant he had read it. As a matter of fact, it did seem rather badly crumpled, as if it had been crushed in a savage grip.

The next letter was different. It had been written to a "Doctor Mornington" who had once been Peaceable's tutor and was still the chaplain and librarian at Thorne. He was also evidently an intelligent and lonely man who had been very much attached to the lonely and intelligent boy. I gathered from the letter that he had been ill, and Peaceable was doing his best to interest and entertain him. He gave a long description of life in New York during the British occupation of the city — so vivid that I could almost smell the mud on the streets and hear the voices of the refugee Tories clamoring at headquarters for rations and firewood — with some highly interesting observations on the underlying causes of the war and the strategic importance of the Battle of Saratoga. This letter had been carefully folded again and tied with narrow library tape. Looking down into the chest, I could see that it was partly filled with almost a hundred other letters of the same kind.

"So *that* was what General Burgoyne really said about Sir Henry Clinton!" Pat exclaimed suddenly. He was stretched out on the floor beside me, papers strewn all around him, and his head bent over one of the brown leather diary books. "Heaven, suppose he'd ever left this lying about on his desk and somebody'd found it! The War Office in London would have blown sky-high. And Peggy! do listen to this one! September fifteenth, 1780, John André asked him out for dinner, 'to inquire into the state of the roads around West Point' — that must have been when he was planning the interview with Benedict Arnold — 'professing great respect for my knowledge and experience, which I told him he might better prove by paying a little more regard to my misgivings about the whole enterprise. He is very contemptuous of the enemy, and overpersuaded that he can buy his way out of any conceivable difficulty by offering a moderate bribe to the rebels, though I warned him that a dishonest American is only infuriated by a *moderate* bribe, and an honest one by any kind. He began to laugh and coax the tavern cat with a bit of the pigeon from his plate; and she came up to him purring; he tossed her the bit of meat and said, "Nonsense! It will be just like this!" — and when I went away, he was still laughing and playing with the cat.' Laughing and playing with the cat — Oh Lord! Can't you see him doing it?"

I thought of the desperate André trying to bribe the three militiamen on the dark road a week later, and shivered. I could not help wondering if he had remembered the cat.

"Fair makes your blood run cold, doesn't it?" said Pat. "Talk about the stuff history's made of! Do you suppose all the rest of it is just as good as this? No wonder your Uncle Enos couldn't bear to part with it! And speaking of Uncle Enos —" he turned his head and scrambled suddenly to his feet, "isn't that somebody out in the library now? It's all right, Dr. Lewis! We've found them."

"That's one blessing, anyway," said the doctor's voice somewhere outside. "He's rational now, and most of the sedative's worn off, but the sooner he stops worrying about those papers, the — Merciful heavens! What have you got in here? Captain Kidd's secret headquarters?"

"Complete with skeleton. We think this must be what he's had on his mind all along. Can we take it up to him now?"

The doctor eyed the chest dubiously.

"You can't very well go dumping all that on his bed," he objected. "One or two of the papers and a book, perhaps. Just enough to show that you've got them. I told him you were here. Make it as short as you can, won't you? He really shouldn't be talking to anybody."

Uncle Enos was propped against the pillows, watching the door with a sort of painful eagerness as we came into the room. He did not say anything, and apparently he did not even see the doctor or me. He was looking at Pat. The rest of us might have been spectators standing unnoticed at the back of the courtroom or lost in the crowd around the foot of the gallows. It really was almost dreadfully like the moment just before a trial or an execution.

Then Pat did something which would probably have made me fall in love with him if I had not fallen in love with him already. He went straight across to the bed without even an instant's hesitation, and put the diary book and the letters down on the coverlet.

"There you are, sir," he said gently. "I was glad to find that they'd been in such good hands."

Uncle Enos straightened up and made an effort to speak. The words came very slowly, as if they were being forced out of him one by one under enormous pressure, but his voice was steady and perfectly clear.

"I beg your pardon," he said. "It was a contemptible thing to do. There was no possible excuse for it."

"You are distressing yourself quite unnecessarily, sir."

"Nothing could be more necessary," said Uncle Enos, still in that steady voice. "If there is any satisfaction that I can give you as a gentleman —"

I saw the corner of Pat's mouth twitch.

"I can't very well offer you a choice of swords or pistols at dawn in Central Park," he observed gravely. "It's this degenerate age we live in. I had thought of asking you if you couldn't see your way to working on them in collaboration with me instead. A little later on, perhaps, when you're stronger?"

Uncle Enos stared up at him incredulously.

"You can't be serious," he whispered.

"I am entirely serious."

"But —"

"They really ought to be kept in the family," Pat added, persuasively.

For some mysterious reason, the word "family" seemed to comfort and reassure Uncle Enos. He drew a long breath of relief and sank back against his pillows. "I suppose they really ought to be," he agreed, in a voice that was suddenly very indistinct and tremulous.

Pat only smiled back at him, and went on standing quietly for a moment beside the bed. Uncle Enos's head sank a little deeper into the pillows, and his eyes closed as if he could no longer keep them open. One hand went out and touched the brown leather cover of the diary book. "Did you see what he said about the plot to discredit Cornwallis?" he murmured drowsily.

"No; not yet. Only the bit about John André and the cat."

"Oh, that's nothing, my boy," Uncle Enos as-

260

sured him, sitting up again immediately. "Wait till you read the entry for the first of June, in '79! The part about André going over to one of Peaceable's rendezvous places near Duck Head's Lake and the man who came out secretly to meet him there. You'll never guess who it was. Not Washington himself, of course, but short of that — well, I could hardly believe it myself. Fortunately, he wanted too much, and Clinton decided to let him go and concentrate on Arnold instead."

"But I thought André was at the capture of Stony Point on the first," Pat objected, dropping down absent-mindedly on the edge of the bed. "Professor Van Doren says in his book —"

"That was only the story they put about. Actually, it seems that André —"

The doctor took an imperative step forward.

"All right, you two," he said. "Break it up. You've got all the rest of your lives to talk history."

It must have been almost half past five when Pat and I finally left the house again and went wandering lazily up through the orchard to bring Betsy down from the gate. The late afternoon light was already beginning to fall through the apple trees in a lovely stillness of green and gold. We walked slowly, taking our time, without trying to say much of anything, and stood leaning against the gate side by side looking down at Rest-and-be-thankful at the foot of the hill, while the stillness deepened and the light stretched out on the grass under the apple trees, as if it too saw no particular reason why the moment should ever come to an end.

"Oh, I forgot to tell you," said Pat. "I took away that signet ring with me just now when we locked up the panel again. I thought it would do for the time being until I can see about getting you the real one. Would you like me to send home for the official Thorne Betrothal Ring, which is a ghastly great object full of sapphires that we haven't been able to sell because it's got to go down in the family, or would you rather I bought you a modest diamond chip with my entire income?"

He took Peaceable's signet out of his pocket and began trying to see if he could balance it on a knothole in the top rail about halfway between us.

"I — I don't know whether we really ought to be thinking about anything like that yet," I murmured. "Y-you said I could have as long as I liked to — to accustom myself to the idea."

"This is only to help you get accustomed to it sooner," said Pat, slipping the ring on my finger and then laying his hand firmly over mine on the top rail to keep me from doing anything about it. "You're not used to being happy, are you, Peggy? Is that what's the trouble?"

"I suppose it is. You don't understand, Pat. I know it's silly. But to be so completely happy, all

of a sudden, when you've never actually been happy for a minute in your whole life — I don't quite know what to do with it. It can't be real. I keep feeling that it will go away if I touch it."

"Wait till you're trying to darn my socks in the deplorable flat behind the red brick university," said Pat. "That'll be real, it will. Mrs. Dykemann says she doesn't understand what it is that I do to them. They won't go away, either. It's all right, my darling. I said you could have as long as you liked. Meanwhile, if you don't mind, I think I will put my arm around you again, so that you can start getting accustomed to that, too."

He put his arm around me again, and we went on leaning against the gate. A little rippling wave of happiness creamed suddenly around my feet, and receded again, and came back more strongly, like a tide beginning to come in on the turn.

"Peggy!" said Pat suddenly.

"Yes."

"There's something I suppose I ought to tell you."

"What is it, Pat?"

Pat did not answer for a moment, and when I glanced up I saw to my surprise that he had turned his head away and was looking down the slope over the apple trees and frowning.

"What is it, Pat? What's the matter?"

"I suppose you could call it a secret."

"This seems to be our day for secrets. What is it?

264

What were you going to tell me?"

"It's about my name."

"But you told me about your name. I've got it all straight now. The title is Thorne, and the family name is Sherwood, and the Christian name is Patrick in full, and — is there anything else?"

"Not exactly — I mean, the trouble is it's not exactly Patrick," explained Pat, confusedly. "I only wish it was. They begin with the same letter, that's all. I made up the 'Pat' myself when I went away to school because I knew what would happen if the other boys ever found out about the real one. I've always hated it. It sounds so silly."

I stared up at him for an instant in complete bewilderment, and then suddenly remembered something and understood.

"Pat! You don't mean to say it can really be —"

"Yes, I'm afraid so," Pat interrupted me hurriedly. "Now you know. I must love you, or I'd never have told you. I've always tried to keep it such a dead secret in the family. Why don't you stay quiet for a bit and just look at the view? You're not going to get a view like that when you're darning a basketful of socks somewhere behind the red brick university."

It was that last moment at the end of a clear summer afternoon when the air is completely still and all the colors seem most rich and intense. Rest-and-be-thankful lay hushed in the silence under the circling curve of the hill and the dark vastness of Martin's Wood. Never had it looked so beautiful, so like a house in a fairy tale caught out of the living world and sleeping away the centuries in some enchanted dream. Through the trees I could see the great chimneys, and the corner of the room in the north gable where Uncle Enos slept, and the yellow roses growing over the long windows that opened on the terrace below. I could see one of the great urns heaped with ivy and rose geranium, and the four figures standing beside it leaning in a cluster against the gray balustrade. The marvelous light caught first the scarlet uniform and then the blue one, the coppery gold of one girl's hair, and the shimmering rose gown of the other. They were looking up at us and laughing. Then the first stir of the evening wind swept the leaves of the apple trees together, and they were gone.

I stood there gazing down at the dreaming house for another long moment. Then quite deliberately I turned around in the circle of Pat's arm, so that the view was completely and most happily limited to his shoulder and the line of his jaw and the way his eyebrows came together in a little frown whenever he was embarrassed or thinking hard about something.

"Tell me about the red brick university, Peaceable," I said.